The Red Rose Box

The Red Rose Box

Brenda Woods

G. P. Putnam's Sons ~ New York

Acknowledgments

I thank God, who always helps me. Special thanks to
Barbara Markowitz, a great agent and good person. She
never stopped believing. Special thanks, also, to Victoria
Wells, Nancy Paulsen, Kathy Dawson, and everyone at
Putnam for their guidance, patience, and clarity.

Published simultaneously in Canada. Printed in the United States of America.
Designed by Gina DiMassi. Text set in Horley Old Style.
Library of Congress Cataloging-in-Publication Data
Woods, Brenda (Brenda A.) The red rose box / Brenda Woods.
p. cm. Summary: In 1953, Leah Hopper dreams of leaving the poverty
and segregation of her home in Sulphur, Louisiana,
and when Aunt Olivia sends train tickets to Los Angeles
as part of her tenth birthday present, Leah gets a first taste of freedom.
[1. Segregation—Fiction.   2. African Americans—Fiction.   3. Sisters—Fiction.
4. Louisiana—Fiction.   5. Los Angeles (Calif.)—Fiction.]   I. Title.
PZ7.W86335 Re 2002 [Fic]—dc21 2001018354 ISBN 0-399-23702-X
3 5 7 9 10 8 6 4 2

To my sons,

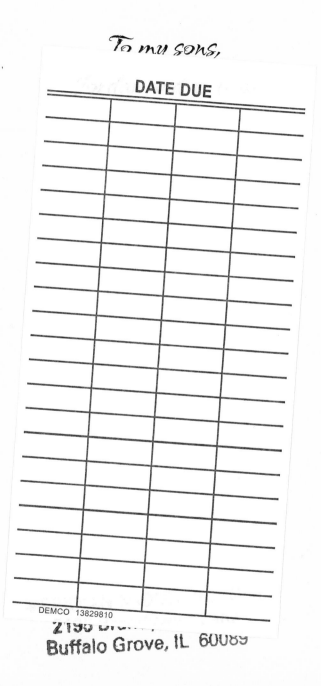

DATE DUE

2195 ...
Buffalo Grove, IL 60089

Part 1

*I would always remember my daddy, tall and brown,
the tenderness in my mama's touch.*

One

The first thing you need to know about the red rose box is that I wasn't expecting anything. I suppose that's when most good things come, when you're not looking.

It was the middle of June 1953, nearly noon, my tenth birthday. Ruth, my sister, was eight. We were sitting out front, Ruth and I, watching the day go by, when Gramma's gentleman friend, Elijah, drove up. Gramma was sitting in the back of his rusty black truck, her legs dangling. She was holding a big box wrapped in brown paper, and we ran up to her, buzzing like bees around a peach tree in bloom, because we thought our third cousin Lettie had sent us more pralines and plum preserves from New Orleans. Gramma stumbled out of the truck and Elijah drove off, not saying anything, like he usually did. All we saw was his brown hand waving.

Ruth tugged on Gramma's worn yellow skirt and asked, "What you got in there?"

Gramma replied, her tone made snappy by the heat, "Nuthin for you," so I just stepped aside.

I ran to the screen door, opened it for Gramma, and walked in after her.

Gramma looked around and asked, "Where's your mama?"

"She gone to Lake Charles with Miss Lutherine, shoppin," I replied. Miss Lutherine was our nosy neighbor.

Gramma sat down and put the box on the front room table. Ruth and I looked and waited. Sweat dripped from Gramma's forehead. She reached in her pocket for her handkerchief, wiped her brow, then the back of her hot, toasted neck, and asked for a cold glass of water. I went to the kitchen because Ruth was too short to reach the faucet and I had longer legs. I filled the glass with water, took two cubes of ice from the icebox, and put them in the glass. The ice crackled, made three pops, and I jumped, startled.

Gramma took the glass from my hand and drank her water slowly like it was a pale green mint julep. I looked at her, then the box, wishing I had four eyes instead of two. She put her glass down, told me to sit next to her, put her hands on my face over my ears, pulled me to her, and kissed my forehead, the way she had a habit of doing to me and Ruth. She said my name twice and it sounded like an echo. "Leah . . . Leah, this is for you . . . from your aunt Olivia."

All I knew about Aunt Olivia, Mama's only sister, was that she lived in California and that she and my mama had stopped talking to each other before I was born and that no one mentioned her name in our house unless they wanted to go home hungry or wearing a frown. Once, Olivia had sent me and Ruth a postcard from Paris and we had taped it to the wall inside our closet.

I tore at the paper. There was a cardboard box underneath. A card was taped to it. The card had a picture of a hot air balloon, red and orange, green and yellow, the kind that floats up high in a clear blue sky. It said "Happy Birthday" on the outside and on the inside Olivia had written some words.

Ruth said, "Lemme see," and stood close to me. Her head touched my shoulder and I smiled at her.

"Dear Leah," I read. "This is a very special gift. It has a lock and key and it's only for you. One day, you will be a woman, a wonderful woman. This is your box of . . ." I didn't know the next word and I asked Gramma for help before I remembered she couldn't read. I tried again. "This is your box of fem-i-ni-ni-ty." I stopped reading and asked Gramma, "What's femininity?"

She replied, "Somethin inside that makes us dif'rent from mens, like Eve was dif'rent from Adam."

I said, "Oh," and read the next line. "Happy birthday to you. Love, Olivia."

I put the card down and Gramma told me to open the box. I opened it, pulled out the packing paper, and didn't expect to see what I did. It was a traveling case with a lock and key, but what made it beautiful was that it was covered with red roses. Nobody who lived way out in the country, who walked the dirt roads in Sulphur, Louisiana, like we did, had ever seen anything like this, let alone had one to call their own. I almost didn't want to touch it. So I put it on the table and stared.

Gramma said, "Open it up, girl. Open it up, Leah Jean."

I put the key in the lock and turned the key and it popped open. Then I looked at Ruth sideways before I lifted the top. If you think the red rose box was something, it's only because you weren't there to see what was in it. In the top of the case there was jewelry. Gramma picked it up in her hands, looked at each piece extra hard, and said, "It ain't real, just costume jewelry, but most folks, even down in New Orleans, would think it is and some would even swear it is."

It didn't matter to me whether it was real or not. All I knew was that it was pretty and that it belonged to me. There was a string of pearls and two pair of earrings. One pair had a pearl and a ball of what looked like real diamonds. The other had three purple stones set in the middle of yellow metal. Ruth touched them with her hand, and I let her because I loved her and her birthday didn't come until four days after Christmas. So if Olivia was going to send Ruth a box, it probably wasn't coming until then.

Gramma took the pearls out of the box and put them around my neck. She smiled and said, "You look all growed up, Leah Jean."

There was a small black jewelry box and I opened it. Inside there was a real watch, not like the ones that get tossed at Mardi Gras by costumed people. It was a watch with a pink band and a white pearly face like the inside of an oyster shell. I saw Gramma's eyes fill up with tears as she helped me wind it, and I went into the kitchen to look at the clock that was sitting high above the stove and set the time. Ruth and I took turns putting it to our ears, listening to it tick, listening to it tock, and we almost forgot about the red rose box. Almost.

Two

The watch, earrings, and pearls would have been enough for me but not for Ruth. I knew because she went over to the red rose box, looking inside for more.

"Ruth!" Gramma fussed.

But by then, Ruth had opened the inside top and was staring into the box like there was a big, fat daddy cockroach inside. I went over to the box and Gramma could tell from the upward curl on the ends of my lips that there was no bug inside. I reached into the box and pulled out something that was store-bought and pink with white lace. Gramma took it from my hands and looked at it all over, even the sewn-in tag.

She told Ruth and me, "Thissa hundred percent silk bed jacket, like a robe, like what rich white womens wears b'fore bed at night when it ain't too cold."

Ruth, still looking in the box, replied, "We ain't kin to no rich white folks."

I paid Ruth no mind, reached in the box, and pulled out a bottle of purple water. The glued-on paper said it was Lavender, Lavender for the Bath. There was another bottle and this one said,

Gardenia, Lotion for the Skin. It seemed like I kept pulling one thing after the other out of the red rose box.

I held up pink satin slippers. Ruth said, "Ooh," and Gramma was still smiling.

But when I pulled out the red nail paint, red lipstick, and two pair of underpants, both with red polka dots, Gramma's smile left her and she said, "Your mama gonna have a fit."

There were only two other things in the box, unless it had a secret place. There was a letter with Mama's name on it and a silk scarf that was white with black flowers.

Gramma said, "Silk and satin good to tie round your hair at night so it won't be wild, stickin up all over in the mornin. Learned that from a white woman I used to work for in Baton Rouge after the war." She tied the scarf around my head and I must have looked like I was ready for Mardi Gras in the bed jacket and slippers, pearls and earrings, when Mama opened the door, our neighbor, Miss Lutherine, behind her.

Mama had both feet over the threshold, Miss Lutherine only one, when one of my earrings fell off. It dropped before I could catch it. Mama looked at me, then Gramma, then Ruth, then at the red rose box, and only one word came from her mouth. "Olivia," Mama whispered.

Mama walked into the kitchen. Miss Lutherine started smiling, and Ruth and I smiled back. Mama put her bags down and closed the kitchen door. Miss Lutherine laughed and we, Ruth and I, couldn't keep from joining her.

Gramma pushed herself up from the sofa and told me, "Take those things off." She went into the kitchen and the door swung shut, sending a warm breeze.

I took everything off, like I'd been told, folded the scarf and the bed jacket, placed them in the red rose box along with everything else except Mama's letter, closed the box, and locked it with the key. I went into our room, Ruth behind me like a shadow at noon, and put the key under the birthday card in the drawer where we kept our underclothes. We opened the closet, pulled the light string once, and closed the door so we wouldn't have to listen if Mama started up. We looked at the postcard from Paris that was still taped to the wall and sat down.

I was wondering what Paris was like, when Ruth broke the spell.

"You oughta go get your box b'fore Mama do somethin with it," Ruth said.

I opened the closet door and tiptoed into the front room where Miss Lutherine was sitting, nosy as always, looking at the box like it was a warm rhubarb pie. I picked it up by the handle, walked back into our room, brought it into the closet, sat down on the floor, and waited. We didn't think we were going to get a whipping, because we didn't ask Olivia to send the red rose box, but we thought that Mama might have heard us giggling. We thought we might be invited out back to pick us a switch from the tree for that, birthday or no birthday.

We sat there for one whole hour. We knew because I had on the real pink watch and Ruth and I both knew how to tell time. It was one o'clock when we opened the closet door and peeked into the front room. Miss Lutherine was gone.

Ruth was sucking her thumb and I pulled it out of her mouth and told her, "Stoppit, cuz your thumb gonna fall off and never grow back. It ain't like no lizard tail." Ruth put her thumb back in her mouth and smiled.

The kitchen door was wide open and Mama and Gramma were cooking. I could tell because the flavors filled the house the way honeysuckle on the vine fills the air around it. We stood in the doorway and watched Mama open the oven door and put the cake tins inside, one chocolate, one vanilla. Gramma was frying chicken. Potatoes and eggs were boiling on the stove for salad.

A pitcher of lemonade sat in the middle of the table, round lemon slices floating at the top like lifesavers from a boat, and Mama said, "Pour you a glass and drink it cuz y'all didn't have no lunch." I poured it hastily and spilled a little but Mama didn't get mad. She kept humming and looked over and told me to get a dishrag. That's when I knew that something had changed.

Ruth got up from the table and went into the front room, looking for the letter. She came back into the kitchen, walked up to Gramma, tugged on her yellow skirt again, and told her, "Miss Lutherine took Mama's letter." Then she tugged on Mama's green-and-white gingham apron string and said, "We was only laughin cuz Miss Lutherine made us."

Mama pulled the letter from the pocket of her apron and told Ruth, "Stop blamin Miss Lutherine." Then she put the letter back in her pocket.

Ruth sat down and we looked at each other hard, grinning because our behinds had been spared. I took a sip of lemonade. It was bittersweet.

"What did the letter from Olivia say?" I asked Mama.

"Aunt Olivia, Leah," she replied.

"What did the letter from Aunt Olivia say?" I asked.

"It was just a short note along with some train tickets," Mama replied.

Ruth asked, "Train tickets? Can we see them?" Mama took out the note, slipped it into her apron pocket, and then let her have the envelope. Ruth took out the tickets, placed them on the table, and counted aloud, "One, two, three, four."

Then I counted them again, "One, two, three, four." I looked at the tickets and remembered what our teacher, Mrs. Redcotton, had told us about the train trip she had taken to Chicago last summer. She called the train a "Jim Crow train" and said that colored had to sit separate from white until they crossed a line. I didn't remember what the line was called but I remembered that she told us that in Chicago there were places where colored could go most anywhere they wanted. She told us that in Chicago there were no white and colored drinking fountains and that colored didn't have to sit in the back of the bus unless they wanted to. She said that in some places white and colored children went to school together. She called it "freedom." I wondered why.

I looked at the tickets closely. They each said New Orleans to Los Angeles. Mama opened the oven door, pulled out one of the cake tins, stuck a toothpick in the middle to see if the cake was done, closed the oven door, and sat down with me and Ruth at the table. Gramma stood at the counter, crying over chopped onions, whistling to radio music.

Mama poured herself a glass of lemonade and I asked her, "Isn't Los Angeles in California?"

"Yes . . . near Hollywood. Your aunt Olivia lives there," she answered.

"Who's goin?" I had two fingers crossed under the table.

She drank the entire glass of lemonade, taking large gulps, before she looked at the tickets and replied, "You, Ruth, Gramma, and me. Daddy cain't cuz he's workin in Houston, be gone till sometime in July. We gonna havta borrow some travlin bags from Sister Goodnight, down the road. I'll sew y'all some new things so you don't look like country ragamuffins, even though that's what folks calls you b'hind your backs, mine too." She kept talking. "Gotta buy a pressin comb and trim your hair. Havta call your daddy, make sure it's all right with him for us to go travlin without him."

Something told me that we were going to go anyway, no matter what Daddy had to say.

Mama's name was Marguerita Ann Hopper but everyone called her Rita. Today Rita Hopper looked happy. She smiled and her dark brown eyes danced around the room.

Three

$\mathcal{M}$ama waved a horsefly away from her face and got up to finish my birthday supper. Ruth and I went outside and sat on the porch swing. We pushed it back and forth, back and forth, the rusty gears keeping time like a choir of crickets.

I told Ruth, "Los Angeles is the most prettiest place on earth and I don't think Mama's gonna take my box from me."

"She might take away the lipstick and the nail paint," Ruth replied.

We were still talking and swinging, swinging and talking when Elijah drove up again. This time he parked his truck in the dirt, got out, took his dusty derby off, and acted like he was going to stay awhile.

He sang, "Happy birthday to you, happy birthday to you . . ."

Gramma came out on the porch and Elijah stopped singing. He was ashamed because he couldn't sing a lick. He went over to Gramma, kissed her on the mouth once, twice, and then Ruth and I were ashamed. Elijah was the only man she'd let come around since her husband, our grandaddy, died, curled up next to her, one Sunday morning just before I was born. She always said that I'd come to take his place, another kind, tender soul.

Elijah and Gramma went inside and I knew that he was in Mama's pots because she ran him out of the kitchen. He came back outside and sat down on the porch step.

That's when I told him, "We's goin to Los Angeles and you gonna have to carry us to New Orleans in your truck."

He paused, the way folks do before they ask a question they're not sure they should be asking, and said, "What was in the box?"

We were just about to tell him when we saw Miss Lutherine and Sister Goodnight walking up the dusty path to our front door, arm in arm.

Sister Goodnight was yellow, plump, pretty. The postman said her real name was Roberta but everyone called her Sister. She wore store-bought clothes, leather shoes, silk stockings with seams, gloves most days, a straw hat in the summertime. She was from New Orleans, where she used to work with some of the other high tones, Creoles, and pretty brown girls, spending time with sailors who had money to spend. Gramma said that was how Sister Goodnight came to have the finest colored house in Sulphur, Louisiana. Gramma called Sister Goodnight a harlot.

I didn't know what a harlot was but one day after school when no one was around, I had asked my teacher, Mrs. Redcotton. She had looked at me in a funny way and replied, "It's not a nice thing to say about a lady."

Elijah always said that Sister Goodnight was still a pretty woman whether it was true or not.

Miss Lutherine was blue black with a wide behind. She was too tall with bowed legs that made her look like she rode horses. Her nose was wide, her eyes big, her fingers too long. Elijah said God must have been on his day off the day Miss Lutherine came to be.

Miss Lutherine smiled. The sun found her and her gold tooth gleamed. She said, "Happy birthday, Leah Jean Hopper," and she and Sister Goodnight kissed me on the cheek. Feather kisses.

Elijah went into the house to get a chair for Sister Goodnight and I heard Gramma ask, "Why you always dotin on that ole dried-up harlot?"

Ruth must have heard too because she asked Miss Lutherine, "Whatsa harlot?"

Miss Lutherine sneezed and the porch shook.

Sister Goodnight wasn't ashamed. She sat down when Elijah brought her the chair and she asked him for a shot of gin. Sister Goodnight knew that Mama didn't keep the devil's brew in her cupboards but she smiled at Elijah and sucked her teeth. Elijah smiled back and went to fetch her a glass of lemonade.

Ruth left the swing and told Sister Goodnight, "You gonna havta let us use your travlin bags cuz we bout to go to Los Angeles, near Hollywood, for the Fourth of July."

Sister Goodnight replied, "You little lyin skunk."

I spoke up. "Ruth ain't no lyin skunk. I am proud to say that we's goin to Los Angeles to see our aunt Olivia."

Sister Goodnight took a sip of lemonade, looked into the setting sun, and said, "Olivia used to dance half naked at the Cotton Club."

Miss Lutherine sneezed again.

I looked straight into Sister Goodnight's hazel eyes and said, "Least she wasn't no harlot."

Silence came over us like the smell of chitlins cooking.

Ruth waited for about ten minutes and quietly asked her if we could still use her traveling bags and Sister Goodnight, after letting my words roll off her back, said yes.

~

We ate supper quietly, the way hungry people do.

"You sure know how to clean a chicken bone, Leah Jean," Miss Lutherine said.

I whispered, "I was hungry cuz I didn't have no lunch," and excused myself from the table. Ruth excused herself and we waited near the open kitchen window while they talked. The hot, heavy, humid air covered us.

"I wish Daddy was here," I whispered to Ruth.

"Me too," Ruth replied.

I knew that if Daddy were here, everyone around that table would be laughing and smiling while he told his tall tales. Daddy would have on a wide grin and talk about how one day he was going to have a big house and a fine car. Mama would shake her head and call him a dreamer. Gramma would tell her to let a man have his dreams because sometimes that was all a colored man had that he could call his own. Daddy's eyes would start to water and Elijah would ask him to tell another tall tale. Daddy would pick up his pipe, light it, and take a few puffs. Then he would tell us about the time he caught a rattlesnake and had it for his supper. I missed my daddy, tall and brown.

~

The table was cleared and Mama put my cake on the table. Ten candles lit the darkened room. Before I blew them out, I made a wish. I wished that I wouldn't spend all of my life in Sulphur. Then I thought and made the same wish for Ruth. I wanted to send Mama a postcard from Paris once, maybe twice. I suppose I was like Daddy, a dreamer. My breath caught all ten candles and they lost their little flames.

Mama cut the cake and I ate two pieces. Ruth ate three because she had a sweet tooth. Miss Lutherine and Sister Goodnight found their way home and we were sent to bed. We kissed Elijah and Gramma, hugged Mama, went into our room, and closed the door.

While we were getting undressed, I told Ruth, "I'm gonna be a teacher, like Mrs. Redcotton."

Ruth rolled her eyes and replied, "You's just like Daddy, Leah . . . silly. Get the key to the red rose box and put on the hundred percent silk bed jacket."

"No," I told her. "I'm savin it for Hollywood." I kept talking. "One day I'm gonna send you a postcard from Paris, France."

Ruth said, "I'm gonna be in Paris, France, with you," and we laughed until our sounds made their way under the door and Mama told us to stop all that noise and turn off the light. I checked under the birthday card to make sure the key was still there, turned off the light, and climbed into the top of the bed. Ruth slept at the bottom and she started wiggling as usual, kicking me with her feet.

I told her, "If you don't stop, I'm gonna throw you off the train and you ain't never gonna see Los Angeles." Then she stopped or fell asleep. I can't be sure which.

Four

Early the next morning, Elijah drove Mama to Lake Charles to buy a few things for the trip and Gramma sat down in our kitchen. She sipped ice water and the sun lit half her face.

I was braiding Ruth's hair into seven braids instead of two.

Gramma told me, "Take all them braids out. Y'all ain't no pickaninnies."

"Mrs. Redcotton says that ain't is not a real word," I said.

"I'm sure Mrs. Redcotton knows what she's talkin bout," she replied.

Ruth asked her, "What's a pickaninny?"

"Gals with more than three nappy braids on their head. More than three nappy braids, that's a pickaninny."

I told her, "Emma Snow got good hair. Her hair don't even need no pressin comb. She still got five or six braids, sometimes seven or eight."

Gramma crossed her legs, took another sip of water, and said, "Still a pickaninny."

"Oh," I replied.

Ruth turned and the comb fell from my hand. She looked into Gramma's eyes and asked, "Why Mama been so mad at her?"

Gramma put down her glass. "Mad at who?"

"Olivia. Mama been so mad and the letter didn't say nuthin but 'I am very sorry.' "

Gramma stirred the water with her finger. Pieces of ice bumped one another, small icebergs in a small ocean. "What y'all doin readin your mama's mail?"

"We was curious," I replied.

Ruth added, "And nosy, too nosy not to. It was peekin outta her apron pocket."

Gramma stood, walked over to the window, pulled the curtains closed like she was trying to keep her words inside, and said, "Bout a man, a winkin man, a smooth man with a smooth voice and a smooth walk like a snake. Rita was lookin after his half-blind mama and I suppose she started longin for him, but when he met Olivia . . . one look was all they needed. Him and Olivia went north on the train, never looked back. Two sisters in love with the same smooth man. Not a bad man, just a ladies' man. Kinda man don't b'long to no one for too long. Got Olivia to New York, took her to Paris, where he left her. Olivia and Rita ain't spoke since. Rita been bitter. Spose she never forgot the smooth man. Boon was his name, part Creole, part not. Some men make a life outta stealin hearts. . . . Olivia said she dun her a favor. Said she wasn't gonna say she was sorry for doin someone a favor. Spose I could understand that. Twelve years . . . took Olivia twelve years to say those words Rita been waitin on. 'I'm sorry.' Twelve years is a long time." She pulled back the curtains and the room filled with light.

Ruth and I didn't say anything.

We went outside and got the washtub and washboard, filled the tub with water and borax, and washed Miss Lilly's clothes like we always did on Saturdays. We rinsed the clothes, hung them to dry, and smiled at each other.

We knew that no man like Boon would ever come between us.

Time blew by and dried the clothes. The day was lazy, hot, sticky summertime and the willows moved with the wind.

"Why cain't Miss Lilly do her own work?" Ruth asked as she walked through the maze of hanging clothes.

"Cuz she got enuf money to pay someone else to do it," I replied.

"I thought it was cuz she's afraid the white might wash off," Ruth said with the devil's grin.

I said, "White don't wash off, black neither."

Ruth laughed.

We had just finished folding the clothes that had been warmed by the sun when Mama and Elijah returned, their arms full. We followed them inside. Mama had bought more dress-making material than I had ever seen in our house and ten new pair of underpants, five for Ruth, five for me.

Mama said, "Throw away all them raggity drawers." She told us we would have to wash our underpants every evening and gave us each a bar of Ivory soap.

Then she gave us each a pair of brand-new black patent leather shoes. She said she bought them big so our feet would have room to grow and stuffed cotton in the toes so they wouldn't slip off our feet. We put them under our bed so we could look at them morning and evening, just to make certain we weren't dreaming.

Then Mama reminded us, "Miss Lilly gonna be spectin her clothes b'fore sundown. Y'all run along."

We replied, one after the other, like two talking birds, "Yes ma'am . . . Yes ma'am," and made our way barefoot over the dirt path that always helped us find Miss Lilly's back door.

Every morning, from Monday to Friday, Mama worked for Miss Lilly. She ironed her clothes, waxed her furniture, shined her silver, and made her supper.

"How old Miss Lilly is?" Ruth asked, letting her side of the clothes basket nearly touch the ground.

"Old as dirt, Gramma says."

"Why she gotta big house and no childrens?"

"I dunno," I told her. "God gives childrens to some, not to others. God knows why, we don't."

I looked up at the darkening sky. A star fell into the dusky blue and staked its claim.

⁓

We walked up Miss Lilly's seven steps quietly, like ghosts, and put the clothes basket down. I knocked three times and waited. Miss Lilly opened the door. Her thin gray hair was held in place by a black hair net. She was wearing a blue-and-white checked dress, gold earrings, pink lipstick, and all of her real teeth. She counted the sheets and pillowcases and said, "Now, let me see where I put my change purse." She left the door wide open and we peered into her kitchen. It was as clean as Miss Lutherine's chitlins and I looked at the cookie jar, wondering what was in it. Miss Lilly limped toward us with her butter-colored change purse in hand.

She picked up one dime with her wrinkled white hand, then another, and placed them in the palms of our waiting hands.

We said, "Thank you, Miss Lilly," being careful to look at her feet and not her face, and made our way down the same seven steps.

We walked down the gritty path and came to Miss Lilly's peach tree. The peaches were ripe, ready to be eaten, some ready to fall to the ground, and so Ruth relieved the tree of a little of its burden by picking the largest, juiciest one she could find.

I said, "It ain't right, takin without askin."

"Nuthin but a peach, Leah. She ain't likely to miss one peach. Not like she gonna come outside and count em every evenin b'fore she goes to sleep. For all she knows a fox coulda got it, carried it off after it fell to the ground." She bit into the peach and it spilled its juices everywhere.

The full moon glowed above and we saw Nathan and Micah Shine walking ahead of us. They went to school with us and lived down the road from Miss Lilly in a house that looked like it was going to fall down whenever a strong wind blew.

I called, "Nathan! . . . Micah!"

They turned and stopped walking. We ran to where they stood, the dimes making sweat in the palms of our hands.

"Wolf gonna get you both, chew you up and spit you out," Micah Shine teased us. He was twelve, and the half Indian from his mama had crawled into him. Daddy swore Indians had eyes everywhere and I thought Micah Shine was handsome as he looked through me. Nathan tugged on Ruth's braids and we walked with them.

We saw a truck coming and got off the path to let it pass. It got close, closer, two headlights blinding us. Then the headlights went off. The truck slowed. I thought it was Elijah until I saw the two white faces.

The man behind the wheel stopped the truck and said, "Four little barefoot country niggers."

Nathan and Micah cowered, hunching their shoulders, the way colored boys had to when this kind of danger came around. Ruth and I looked straight down into the dust and we all kept walking. Fear walked with us. The man behind the wheel spat on the ground, laughed, and drove on. We turned and watched as the red taillights disappeared like red stars into the darkness.

Micah stood up straight and whispered, "I woulda said somethin. . . . I woulda but I don't wanna wind up hangin from no tree, burned to a crisp."

I looked up, and a gray owl flew in front of the moon.

Nathan and Micah took the path to their house without saying another word and Ruth and I ran home. Afraid.

We planted the peach pit, hoping this one would grow and bear fruit. We were rich until tomorrow, Sunday, when we would drop our shiny dimes into the offering basket along with the other pennies, nickels, quarters, and a few fifty-cent pieces. Sometimes I looked at that money thinking we needed it more than God, but I never told anyone my thoughts. I was certain that kind of thinking would land me in hell or somewhere close.

So that night, I got out my rosary and put it around my neck before I went to bed.

Of course Ruth said, "Don't no rosary b'long round your neck."

I kicked her hard under the covers.

The sun knew when to rise, the moon when to glow, lightning where to strike once, maybe twice.

It was Tuesday and Ruth and I sat in the back of Elijah's truck, scarves tied around our hair. The sun had just come up and as he drove we felt every bump in the dirt road. Elijah stopped his truck. We had come to the cotton fields, ready to work for two dimes, maybe two quarters. At least twice a week during the summer, Ruth and I found ourselves here. I looked at the tips of my fingers, knowing a little blood was about to flow. It was like touching the tiny thorns of a new rosebush, except the cotton plant wasn't pretty to look at. We took our burlap sacks and Ruth, Elijah, and I found a row. Elijah started picking and singing, picking and singing, Ruth and I behind him, picking, just picking. I tried to be careful not to stick my fingers but I always did and it always hurt.

"Ouch," I said, rubbing the tip of my bloody finger on my dress.

Elijah said, "Hurry along, Leah. The skin on your fingers gonna get thick like mine, then you won't have nuthin to whine about."

I looked at my hands. "I'm gonna be a schoolteacher, not no cottonpicker."

"A schoolteacher. You don't say," was his reply.

"She's like Daddy . . . dreamin," Ruth added.

I looked at a tired old woman in the next row, reached toward the prickly plant, took hold of a piece of the white fluff, pulled at it without sticking my fingers, and placed it in the burlap sack.

Elijah was ahead of me, singing and picking when he looked

back at me. "A schoolteacher? Who gived you that idea, Leah Jean?"

"It just come to me one day when I was watchin Mrs. Redcotton write on the blackboard. Mrs. Redcotton said I'm smart enuf. She went to college, so she oughta know."

"You don't say." Elijah bent over, singing and picking.

I thought about the red rose box and the postcard from Paris, a train that was about to take me far away, all the while picking and picking until my sack was nearly full.

I was tired when Ruth and I climbed into the back of Elijah's truck at the end of the day, but there were two quarters in my hand and two in Ruth's. I fell asleep.

The days and nights kept coming and Mama and Gramma stayed up late, cutting dresses, sewing, talking, their low laughter coming in under our door, and by the end of the week we had a closet full of clothes. Mama borrowed a few of what Sister Goodnight called her finer things and by the twenty-ninth day of June, we were in the back of Elijah's truck, on our way to New Orleans. I had the red rose box in my lap, hundred percent silk bed jacket and all.

Elijah let us off in front of the station with our bags, saying he was going to park, but when I saw his hand waving, I knew he was on his way.

I reached down and dusted off my patent leather shoes until I could see myself.

I looked around and around at everything and everybody until it felt like my head was spinning. A porter, high yellow and as polite as could be, came up behind Mama and asked her if she needed a little help. She told him we were going to Los Angeles and he asked to see our tickets. He winked at Mama, smiled at me, piled our trunk on a cart, and tried to take my red rose box. I told him I could carry it myself and I could tell he didn't know that we were poor and country. I followed Mama up four steps into the colored section on that Jim Crow train.

Mama and Gramma took their seats and Gramma put a quarter in the palm of his hand. He seemed thankful as he tipped his hat and walked away, humming a tune. Ruth and I were looking after him when the train started to move. We hurried to the window and stood, looking and watching. We were wearing matching pale blue sundresses with ruffled sleeves. Our hair was fresh and pressed with a warm comb.

I looked at Mama and I thought that she was pretty. I stood in front of her until she reached for me, put her arms around me, and sat me in her lap like a half-grown pig. Mama began to cry and tears rolled down her cheeks.

Gramma shook her head. "Why you cryin, Rita Ann?"

Mama replied through her tears, "Cuz I ain't never wanted nuthin, just a little house, a good husband, and some babies."

Gramma reached for her hand. "Ain't nuthin wrong with bein content, if that's the way you was put together." Then she said, "Lord have mercy, Lord have mercy, Lord have mercy," and Mama stopped crying. Gramma said to me with two quick winks, "Hand me my shoe box, Leah Jean."

I handed her the shoe box, Gramma opened it, offered me a piece of fried chicken, Ruth a piece of stick-it-together cake,

Mama some roasted peanuts, and we ate. I sat in the window seat, watching the world go by. I pictured my daddy. Thinking about him made me smile.

Three days later, we were in Los Angeles.

I was never going to be the same.

Five

*A*unt Olivia walked through the crowd like she was walking on water, and no one had to tell me it was her. She was the prettiest woman in the station, white or colored, at least I thought so. Olivia and Mama looked at each other for what seemed like a long time but no words passed between them. Ruth and I stood together, holding hands. Too many people were weaving in and out, out and in. I kept one hand on Gramma's blue polka-dot dress.

Finally, Olivia, being the oldest and the wisest, reached for Mama and pulled her close. I could see Mama's hurt melt like butter in the sun. I looked at Olivia, and she must have felt my eyes on her soul because she let go of Mama, reached down, touched my shoulder, and kissed my cheek, then the top of Ruth's head. She gave Gramma a hug and a kiss. Then she put her arms around Ruth and me and we walked through the station.

I paused to look at the drinking fountain as we made our way to the door. I was thirsty and there were no signs. I pointed to it and asked Aunt Olivia, "That for white or colored?"

"Anyone who's thirsty, white or colored. No Jim Crow here."

I turned the handle and the cool water met my lips.

We walked to Aunt Olivia's car. It was shiny blue and gleamed in the sun. A porter, who had a face like the man on the Cream of Wheat box, placed our things in the trunk, and as he took his tip with a smile, we got in.

Olivia drove slowly and it was a long ride, through streets full of people, some colored, most not.

Gramma said, "I cain't wait to get outta this girdle, into a housecoat. Lord have mercy, I hate to be uncomfortable."

I looked out of the window, the red rose box in my lap, for ten minutes, according to my real watch. Then I turned and looked at my mama's sister, Olivia. She had dark brown hair, pressed and perfect, red lips and nails, no other face paint, the whitest teeth, skin the color of a sweet praline, delicate bones, and brown almond eyes that didn't dance.

We passed a red streetcar and I looked to see if colored were sitting in the back but I saw a lady with skin so black it was almost purple sitting right behind the driver, and I began to see what Mrs. Redcotton had talked about. We drove past a movie theater but there was no colored entrance, and we passed shops and restaurants, where there were no Whites Only signs. I started to think about the word *freedom*.

When the car stopped, we were in front of Aunt Olivia's house. It was white with green shutters and two stories, and had a brick path, like a house where Mama had once worked in Lake Charles. Olivia called to me and Ruth, and she held our hands while we walked up the steps with her. There were six steps. I know because I counted them.

A round colored lady, dressed like a housemaid, black dress

with a stiff white apron, opened the door. She wore a big smile, a black hair net, no gold teeth, and she called Aunt Olivia "Mrs. Chapel." She was dark brown and her ears were pierced.

She said, "Evenin, Mrs. Chapel."

Olivia replied, "Evenin, Mrs. Pittman. These are my nieces, Leah and Ruth Hopper." Olivia turned to Mama and Gramma and continued her introductions. "And my mother, Mrs. Carter, and my sister, Marguerita . . . Rita Hopper."

"Leah, Ruth, Mrs. Carter, Mrs. Hopper, pleased to meet you. I'm called Mrs. Pittman round here, though I ain't got no mister to speak of." Mrs. Pittman held the door open and we walked through, into another world.

While the grown-ups' minds and eyes were on one another, Ruth and I wandered off. We looked but didn't touch because everything was too fancy. It seemed like no one touched anything and we weren't about to start.

There was a long violet velvet sofa. Two chairs, the color of cream, had threads of gold that made them glisten in the sunlight. In the corner there was one large violet velvet chair with a footrest that matched. Glass lamps with pale yellow shades sat on tables of dark polished wood. The floors were covered with rugs that my feet sank into. There were paintings on the walls surrounded by frames of gold and a staircase with a white banister that curved its way upward. Beauty was everywhere and I liked the way it felt. Ruth took my hand and we smiled at each other as I led her to the foot of the stairs. We looked up, silent, like two cats waiting.

Mrs. Pittman came up behind us and we almost jumped out of our skins.

She said, "Y'all must be tired. I'll show you upstairs to your room so's you can get freshed up."

We walked up those fifteen steps and she took us to a room where everything was pink, including the walls. Mrs. Pittman brought in our traveling bag and left it inside the door. She showed us the bathroom that was attached to the room and it was pink too.

Mrs. Pittman told us as she stood in the doorway, "Mrs. Chapel fancies pink. Mr. Chapel be home soon and you oughta be dressed, ready for supper by then."

She closed the door and we took our shoes off and jumped, like grasshoppers, on the bed that was big enough for two. Ruth went into the bathroom, flushed the indoor toilet, and turned on the water in the tub.

I made her stop. "We don't have time for no bath. Change your drawers and wash up in the sink."

We washed our faces, necks, arms, legs, and ears with pink washcloths that we were afraid to get dirty, put on clean underpants, white undershirts, never worn, matching lavender dresses, clean white socks, and our patent leather shoes. I combed Ruth's hair, braided it into two braids, then combed and braided mine. We sat on the bed, waiting. We didn't know what else to do.

We sat for ten minutes before Mrs. Pittman knocked on the door.

"Come in," I said like a lady. Ruth looked at me out of the corner of one eye.

Mrs. Pittman asked, "Where's your dirty clothes? I'm gonna wash em."

I told her, "We put em in our travlin bag."

"They's called suitcases, not travlin bags." She opened the suitcase, took out the dirty clothes, and told us to take off the lavender dresses because she was going to press them. We did as we were told.

I sat on the bed, a living statue, still as could be, but Ruth, who never knew how to be still, got up, opened the door, and looked after Mrs. Pittman the way folks look after a pretty woman on her way to communion. I told her, "Sit down and be still, like we was told."

Ruth replied in her sassy way, "Ain't nobody told us to sit still."

"Stop sayin ain't," I said.

Ruth frowned. "Didn't nobody tell us to sit down and be still, unless you was hearin things."

I got weak like a twice-used tea bag and followed Ruth into the hallway.

We could hear Mama and Gramma across the way and we tiptoed over to their door, our ears pressed close. Ruth sneezed and Mama opened the door and asked, "What in the world y'all doin in your underclothes?!"

"Mrs. Pittman took our dresses cuz they was wrinkled. That's why," I replied.

Mama said, "Come in quick and close the door."

Gramma was on the bed, slip on, girdle off. The ceiling was painted white but there was pasted-on paper with yellow flowers in bloom everywhere else. I sat on the bed next to Gramma, Ruth in a yellow chair by the window.

Gramma whispered, as if the walls had ears, "Mr. Chapel is a man with a little money."

I asked, "How much money?"

Mama answered, "He's a well-off man who married Olivia cuz she's beautiful."

Ruth, smiling like she was being tickled from the inside, said, "He married Olivia cuz he pro'bly see'd her dancing half naked at the Cotton Club." Then Ruth started dancing around the room like a wild pig and Gramma had a fit.

"Where you heard such nasty nonsense?" she asked Ruth, her voice raised.

Ruth stopped dancing. "Sister Goodnight," she replied.

Gramma pinched Ruth hard enough to make her scream and told her she was going to have to learn to keep her big mouth shut. That's one thing about Ruth; I loved her but she did have a big mouth.

Mama said, "Olivia never danced half naked."

Ruth rubbed her behind where Gramma had pinched her.

Someone knocked on the door and Mama said, "Come in."

~

Mrs. Pittman opened the door, lavender dresses swinging on two wooden hangers, and said, "Good evenin. Mr. Chapel's home and supper's near ready."

We followed her back to the pink room and dressed when she excused herself.

Ruth said, "Mr. Chapel must be a white man."

"No, white cain't marry colored," I told her. When Ruth asked me why, I told her, "Cuz."

We sat on the big bed, bouncing, singing silly songs, until Mama turned the glass doorknob, opened the door, poked her

~

head in, and told us, "Come on downstairs with me." She smiled and said, "You sure are two pretty little gals." That's what Daddy always called us, pretty little gals.

Mama had on lipstick, stockings, a red dress, and Sister Goodnight's real gold earrings, and Ruth and I looked at her for a while because she had her femininity. It must have been something Olivia's house was full of. Mama walked down the steps with what Elijah would have called a sassy wiggle, me and Ruth on her heels. That was when we saw him.

He was puffing on a fat cigar, sitting in the violet velvet chair, the newspaper in his lap. He, Mr. Chapel, looked up, smiled, and winked at the same time. He was so handsome.

I could tell from looking at him that he had some Indian blood. He had clear, dark, red brown skin, black hair, brown eyes, and a shiny, trimmed black mustache. He stood up, taller than my daddy, like a gentleman should, shook Mama's hand, and introduced himself as Bill, Bill Chapel. I watched and thought that I had never seen my mama, Rita Hopper, look at any man except my daddy the way she was looking at Mr. Bill Chapel. The smooth man Boon crossed my mind.

He let go of Mama's hand, patted the tops of our heads, and said, "Sure is nice to have a house fulla beautiful colored women-folk."

Aunt Olivia glided in from the dining room, Gramma on her arm, told us dinner was ready, and looked straight into her husband's twinkling eyes. Mr. Bill Chapel took Mama's arm and Aunt Olivia didn't seem to mind. Ruth and I, holding hands again, followed.

The candlelit dining-room table was set with dishes, match-

~

ing forks, knives, and spoons, water glasses full of cool water, wineglasses waiting to be filled, and ten white roses in a vase, right in the middle. Ruth and I were given seats across from each other and we looked and peeked around those roses, making faces, most of the evening. The plates were white and Ruth picked hers up, admiring her reflection. Gramma pinched her again.

Mrs. Pittman, polite and smiling, came around the table, putting food on our plates, and I felt funny inside, being served.

Mrs. Pittman asked, "Turkey or ham?"

I said, "Turkey and ham."

I looked at Aunt Olivia, who smiled and said, "You must be hungry after that long train ride."

Ruth raised her hand and said, "I want ham and turkey too."

Mr. Chapel said, "Everybody's gonna have ham and turkey, whether they want it or not." Everyone sitting at the table was smiling, and that was when I knew that money was not the root of all evil like Mama and Miss Lutherine were always saying.

We finished eating, Mrs. Pittman cleared the table without any help from us and gave us each a dish with two scoops of what looked like orange ice cream. Mrs. Pittman saw my question before I could speak and said, "Peach sherbet."

Ruth looked around the table. "My nose itches. I smell peaches. Somebody's coming with a hole in his britches." I was waiting for Gramma to pinch her again, but Gramma kept smiling as the silver spoon carried the orange delight to her lips.

I spilled my last spoonful of sherbet on the front of my dress and excused myself from the table, the way Daddy always made us do. I walked up the stairs, through the pink room, into the pink bathroom, and tried to wash the stain from my dress. I scrubbed until the stain was as gone as it was going to be, used the indoor toilet, sat on the bed, and looked around the room. I sat quietly, thinking that I didn't want to ever leave this house with the big bed, fifteen steps, and white roses.

I was still thinking when Ruth came in and told me that she had been sent to bed.

"What you did?" I asked.

"Nuthin," Ruth replied.

"I don't hardly believe you," I said.

I looked at Ruth, her golden eyes, the dark skin, her rust-colored hair, and shook my head. Ruth smiled, knowing I knew the truth, went into the bathroom, put the stopper in the drain, and started running the water. I opened the red rose box, found the lavender bubble water, took the bottle into the bathroom, and poured two capfuls under the running water just like it said.

I told Ruth, "You take a bath first and be careful not to get your hair wet cuz it's gonna go back if you do." I went to get my scarf and when I came back Ruth was in the tub, bubbles every-where.

My sister, Ruth Louise, always had a good time. From the time when she was just a little something, no matter what, even after a whipping, Ruth came in smiling. We were different. Always would be.

I sat on the floor, waiting my turn, but Ruth stayed in the tub so long that I nearly fell asleep and forgot about taking a bath. Ruth got out of the tub and said, "Leah, you ought not go to bed stinkin cuz the sheets is clean."

Ruth wrapped a pink towel around her, looked at herself in the mirror, smiled, and walked out of the bathroom like she was some kind of Mardi Gras queen or Cleopatra.

I had one foot in Ruth's dirty water when she peeked in and said, "Mr. Chapel got enuf water for bout seventeen tubs." I got in her water anyway. There were still plenty of bubbles.

I washed good, even my ears. There was a ring in the tub when the water finished draining, so I put soap on the washcloth and wiped it clean. I put on my white cotton nightgown, clean under-pants, and the hundred percent silk bed jacket. When I went into the bedroom, Ruth was asleep at the foot of the bed. I went to the other side, turned back the sheet, took off the bed jacket, folded it neatly, and put it on the night table. I kneeled by the side of the bed and asked God to take care of my daddy and to send me a husband like Mr. Chapel. I made the sign of the cross, got into bed, put my head on the pillow, and the sandman took me.

Six

*W*hen I opened my eyes, Ruth was staring at me, her broad nose touching mine. I almost forgot where I was. Ruth stood up, shook her narrow hips, and said, "Little Leah Hopper, sittin in a saucer. Rise, Leah, rise. Wipe your winkin eyes."

"Weepin, not winkin," I corrected her.

"So, it don't matter none no way," Ruth replied.

I got up, went to the window, and looked outside. The sun was barely up and the sky was half lit like a room with one candle. I told Ruth to go back to bed.

She said, "No. I smell bacon, biscuits, and somethin sweet."

I didn't have to take a deep breath to know she was right because my sister, Ruth, had a nose for food. She could stand outside any kitchen and name every dish about to be put on the table. Collard greens, corn bread, every kind of gravy, red beans and rice, fried cabbage, catfish, bread pudding, oxtail soup, black-eyed peas and neck bones, grits, okra gumbo, or peach cobbler. Ruth knew.

I put on my bed jacket and pink slippers and opened the door, leading the way, Ruth behind me. We walked down the steps, through the dining room, right up to the swinging kitchen door, pushed it opened just to peek, and saw Mrs. Pittman cutting biscuits from dough with the rim of the glass, like Mama did. Mrs. Pittman turned around, saw my eyes, and welcomed us into her kitchen.

She sat us down, gave us each a cup of cold milk, two warm biscuits with butter and peach preserves, and said, "Mr. Chapel fancies peaches."

She was humming a tune I'd heard Sister Goodnight sing, about bringing in the sheaves, and told us to bless our food. I blessed my food, wondering what sheaves were, butter dripping everywhere.

Ruth asked, "How come Mr. Chapel got a little money?"

"Mr. Chapel was the chauffeur for a rich white man," Mrs. Pittman said. "Then he got rich hisself when he bought up property after the depression for a dollar here, another dollar there. When his first wife died from tuberculosis, every single highfalutin woman from here to New York was on his doorstep, knockin loud for bout two years. He didn't pay most of em no never mind till he ran into Mrs. Chapel at one of his apartments where she was lookin to rent." Mrs. Pittman kept talking. "He been a happy man since that October evenin when he came into the house whistlin 'Honeysuckle Rose.' Now Mr. Chapel and Mrs. Chapel work together. They call it Chapel and Chapel Real Estate."

The last word was barely out of her mouth when Mr. Chapel came into the kitchen through the swinging door, asking for coffee with cream. He saw us, smiled, and asked, "How the little ladies doin?"

We replied, "Fine," and smiled back at Mr. Bill Chapel and then at each other.

He drank his coffee standing up and said good-bye. I went to the window to look after him. He got in his car and drove off.

Ruth asked for some bacon and Mrs. Pittman let her have a piece. She must have read my mind because she gave me a piece too, thick rind and all.

Mrs. Pittman smiled, put the last pan of biscuits in the oven, and started scrambling eggs. She put eggs, fried potatoes, and two slices of bacon on our plates. She gave us more biscuits, poured us some orange juice, and said she was going to fatten us up.

She was still smiling and grinning, grinning and smiling when Mama and Gramma came through the door, nostrils wide open from the smell of food that had filled the house.

Gramma said, "The smell of melted butter on hot biscuits woke us." She wiped the sleep from her eyes and yawned without covering her mouth, and Mama nudged her. Gramma continued, "I'm gonna need some real strong coffee, two cups, if I gotta put up with Rita under the same roof as me for two weeks."

"Where's Olivia?" Mama asked, letting Gramma's words fly by.

Mrs. Pittman replied quietly like a church whisper, "Mrs. Chapel don't eat no breakfast since she lost her babies, two in a row."

We all stopped eating. Mama and Gramma stared into the hiding places of each other's eyes. Then Mrs. Pittman said, "Doctor said she can't have no more. Not even to try is what he made Mr. Chapel promise. Stillborn, first a boy, then a girl . . . beautiful children . . . but none of the Lord's breath was in em."

I expected Mama to make me and Ruth leave the room like she usually did when secrets began to be spoken. Maybe because we were eating in someone else's kitchen, sleeping between someone else's starched sheets, she let us stay. Silence covered us.

⁓

Olivia breezed through the door, wearing lipstick and a smile, and no one said a word. More silence.

Mrs. Pittman, head lowered from telling someone else's secrets, said only, "Mornin," poured a cup of coffee, and offered it to Olivia.

That's when I knew why Olivia's eyes danced only when she looked into her husband's eyes. They had swallowed the same sorrow.

I caught her eyes, smiled into them, and said, "Mornin."

⁓

Gramma got up from the table and excused herself from the kitchen, eyes watering, ready to spill over. Mama kept her tears and began talking about the sights we were going to see. Olivia sat down in Gramma's warmed-up chair, poured some cream into her coffee, then a spoonful of sugar, and sipped. She looked up at Mrs. Pittman and asked for a biscuit, bacon, and two eggs, sunny-side up. Mrs. Pittman looked at Olivia like she was hearing things.

I took one last bite of bacon, excused myself from the table, and took my plate and glass to Mrs. Pittman at the sink. Ruth asked if she could have another biscuit and I went through the swinging door.

The morning lit the house through many windows, and I

found my way to the front room and sat on the velvet sofa. I ran my fingers across it. It was smooth and soft. The big window was made of stained glass, yellow, green, red, blue. The glass lamp on the table in front of the window had hanging crystals that caught the sun and covered the wall with shreds of light. It felt like I was in heaven.

I looked down at my pink slippers. When I looked up, Ruth was standing in front of me, biscuit crumbs sitting in the corners of her mouth.

"You need to wipe your mouth," I told her.

She wiped her mouth with her hands, laughed, and joined me on the sofa. "Why you sittin here?"

"Cuz I want to."

"Oh."

I looked around, studying the room, so that I could take the memory home with me.

Then Ruth and I had the same thought at the same time and we found ourselves looking into every corner of that room, peeking in closets, opening and closing drawers quietly like thieves.

There was a bookshelf with what looked like hundreds of books and I looked through some of them. They weren't library books. I could tell. There were three Bibles and a set of encyclopedias.

Ruth found a tiny bathroom with nothing but a sink and a toilet. She pulled down her underpants and sat on the toilet without closing the door.

"You gotta close the door, Ruth." It was the same thing she did in Sulphur, leaving the outhouse door open, saying she was afraid she might fall in and get covered with lime. I heard the toilet flush.

"Wash your hands, nasty," I said.

"You sure can get on my nerves, Leah. You sure can." Ruth turned on the water in the clean white sink and washed and dried her hands. I would do my business later, upstairs, when no one else was around, like I always did at home, looking through the half-moon cut out in the outhouse door at the sky, blue, gray, or midnight black.

The high-pitched bark of a dog drew us to an open side window. He was a little dog, smaller than a fox, shorthaired, and we heard a lady from the house next door call him "Chili." She spoke a different language. The words sounded like a melody.

"Chili," I called softly. The word floated through the air and found him. He stopped barking, sat back on his hind legs, opened his mouth, and howled.

I looked at my pink watch. It was only nine o'clock but it felt like I had been here for a long time, in this house where the dog next door was named Chili.

Ruth and I walked through the hall toward the back of the house and I opened the back door. Flowers of every color filled the yard and I wondered if I had found the Garden of Eden. I took Ruth by the hand and we walked down the brick steps into the yard. I touched a drying white rose and its petals fell to the ground. The door creaked and we looked toward the back porch where Aunt Olivia stood smiling, her hair loose, brushing her shoulders. She looked like a princess in a pink satin robe.

"Enjoying my flowers, I see," she said.

"Yes ma'am," we said at the same time.

"Call me Aunt Olivia," she said.

"Yes ma'am, Aunt Olivia."

She joined us in her garden and told us that the vine that crept along the back wall with red flowers that looked like tissue paper was called a bougainvillea, that the bush with the big yellow flowers was called hibiscus. I wondered if she would test us later to see if we remembered.

I touched the tip of an orange-and-yellow flower. "What's this?"

"Bird-of-paradise." She gently brushed the hair back from my face and I looked into her eyes. She picked two yellow flowers from the hibiscus bush and tucked one behind my ear and one behind Ruth's. She told us that there were places on some islands where the women wore flowers in their hair and skirts made of grass.

Ruth smiled and said, "You is a very silly woman, Aunt Olivia . . . skirts cain't be made from grass."

Aunt Olivia swore it was so as we made our way back into the house. Gramma and Mama were in the kitchen. Ruth and I walked upstairs to our bedroom, yellow flowers in our hair. Mrs. Pittman was making the bed.

"Y'all look bout ready for Hawaii." Mrs. Pittman fluffed the pillows.

"Where's Hawaii?" I asked.

"Islands in the Pacific Ocean . . . Pearl Harbor . . . where the Japanese bombed us during World War Two."

"It's not part of the United States of America?" I said.

"No, little ma'am, not yet." Mrs. Pittman finished making the bed and told us we should get dressed.

Ruth told her, "Leah's tryin to be a smarty-pants."

"Nuthin wrong with that," was her reply. "Nuthin wrong with that."

~

We ate lunch in the backyard on furniture that stayed outside. I ate my ham sandwich and crunched my potato chips slowly, washing them down with sips of Coca-Cola from the bottle. I was glad Aunt Olivia and Mama had made up; not only had Aunt Olivia been missing from Mama's life, but I felt like she'd been missing from mine.

It was the third day of July and the next day we were going to the beach. The only beach I'd ever been to was Lake Ponchartrain, where we rode for hours to swim in the murky water, passing whites-only beaches all along the way.

"Is the beach here for colored?" Ruth asked Aunt Olivia.

The grown-ups looked around the table at one another.

"No, Ruth," Aunt Olivia replied. "There are no segregated beaches in California."

"What's segregated?" Ruth asked.

"When they tell colored where they can or can't go, to eat, to school, to live, to die," Aunt Olivia answered.

"Like home, like Sulphur," I added.

"Like everywhere beneath the Mason-Dixon line," Aunt Olivia replied.

That was the name of the line Mrs. Redcotton had talked about, the Mason-Dixon line.

"Where's the Mason-Dixon line?" I asked.

Aunt Olivia answered, "Boundary between Pennsylvania and

~

Maryland, separating the North from the South. Won't catch me on the wrong side of that line again. . . . Won't ever catch me."

I was learning about the South, sitting at a table in the North.

The next day Ruth and I approached the blue water of the Pacific Ocean for the first time and I put my foot cautiously in the cool water where white children, men, and women splashed and smiled. I took a deep breath and waded in the water up to my knees, holding Ruth's hand, looking toward the horizon. Freedom.

Later, as we roasted hot dogs on coat hangers over a fire pit, Ruth said hot dogs looked like what she'd seen once between Nathan Shine's legs when he ran out of the house butt naked, his wild-eyed mama chasing him with his daddy's wide belt. I looked at the hot dog, put on some mustard and a little relish, and ate.

I thought about what Micah Shine had said, about not wanting to wind up hanging from a tree. When we got home I was going to tell him that he wouldn't have to worry about being burned to a crisp in Los Angeles, California, near Hollywood, where colored didn't have to sit in the back of the bus unless they wanted to.

The fireworks lit the night sky as we sat on a blanket in the sand and roasted marshmallows, brown, sticky, sweet.

The ocean breeze was cool and smelled of salt and seaweed. I turned to look at Mama and Aunt Olivia. They were alike but different, Olivia delicate, Rita sturdy, both quick to smile, quick to laugh.

Music played and I got up to dance under the moon.

Ruth said, "You cain't dance. It's what everyone says about you, even Mama 'n Daddy."

"Can too." I clapped my hands, keeping time, my head bobbing. Mama and Aunt Olivia, Gramma, and Uncle Bill looked at me and smiled. "See," I said.

"See what?" Ruth rolled her eyes.

I snapped my fingers, "See me dance." I was free, at that moment, in that place.

That night, as I washed the sand and salt from my body in a tub filled with bubbles, thoughts made circles in my mind. Colored go to the back door. No colored allowed. Whites only. Nigger. Go to the back of the bus. Nigger. In Sulphur, it was the way we lived, the way it was.

The next day Mama and I sat in the backyard on the brick steps, under the shade of a tree. It was hot. She took my hand in hers and a summer breeze cooled us.

"Why we gotta go back? I like it here." I was looking for answers.

"Daddy . . . our little house." Her answers sounded like questions.

"Daddy would come, once we tell him bout it. He could get a job here. Daddy would wanna come. I know he would. Then he could buy us a big house and drive a fine car just like he's always talkin bout." She dropped my hand.

"It's what we got. . . . It's what we got, Leah." Nothing else was said.

All I could wonder was why any colored man or woman would ever go back to the South, below the Mason-Dixon line, after knowing what freedom felt like.

———

We ate lunch and drove to a movie theater where we saw Marilyn Monroe in *How to Marry a Millionaire.*

Driving downtown to Chinatown, Mama stared from the window in silence as Gramma and Olivia, Ruth and I chirped and chattered about diamonds being a girl's best friend.

"Sure wish I had some diamonds to call my best friend. A diamond necklace might keep me good company." Gramma looked over at Olivia and smiled.

I said, "Diamonds cain't be your best friend."

"And why is that, Leah Jean?" Gramma asked.

"Cuz they cain't listen to your secrets."

Aunt Olivia looked at the diamond ring on her finger and said, "You're right about that, Leah."

Ruth said, "Leah's my best friend . . . and my sister. I listen to all her secrets."

Olivia parked the car and looked over at Mama, and smiles came to their lips.

In the restaurant, I didn't know what I was supposed to do with the two wooden sticks they gave us with our food.

"They're chopsticks," Aunt Olivia said. She handled them like an expert, picking up rice that was covered with a salty brown liquid called soy sauce.

Mama, Ruth, and I tried but failed, and finally asked for forks. Gramma looked at the shrimp fried rice, shook her head, and jabbed a shrimp with the tip of the stick. Carefully she brought it to her mouth. Then she asked for a fork too. I broke open my fortune cookie. It said, "You will always have good luck and overcome many hardships." Ruth's said, "You will meet a tall, dark stranger." I tucked mine into my sock and Ruth gave hers to Mama to keep in her pocketbook. The people who served us had dark narrow eyes and pin-straight black hair. I knew where they were from. China was in Asia.

Someday, I thought, I will go there. Someday.

Three days later, with tears in our eyes, we were back on the train, bound for New Orleans, the red rose box in my lap.

Seven

*S*eems like as soon as we finished waving good-bye to Aunt Olivia and Uncle Bill Chapel, we were waving hello to Daddy and Elijah. They were waiting inside the train station with their hats on, grinning. I was so happy to see them.

Ruth and I got in the back of Elijah's truck with Daddy, curled up beside him like two snakes under a river rock, and fell asleep.

When I woke, I was in my bed, Ruth tucked in at the foot, Daddy standing over me. I thought I was dreaming. Being close to him almost made me forget about California and chopsticks.

He said, "Seems like your mama dun gone off to Hollywood and got a little fulla herself."

I said, "No, Mama isn't the only one, we's all a little fulla ourselves."

Daddy said with half a smile, "Long as y'all know how to come back down to earth, I ain't bout to worry."

I replied, "Daddy, ain't isn't no real word. That's what Mrs. Redcotton says."

Daddy smiled a big smile, a funny look in his eyes, and said, "Well, you tell Mrs. Redcotton that Willie Hopper said thank you very much for educatin my children to speak proper English." He paused. "I can see now that Leah's on her way to better things."

Ruth added, "Me too."

"Daddy, could we move to California? It's real pretty and they don't have no Whites Only signs and no hurricanes neither. Least that's what Uncle Bill Chapel said." I was trying to convince him.

"Got earthquakes though, plenty of those." Daddy caressed the top of my head.

"What's a earthquake?" Ruth asked.

"The earth begins to shake and rumble, opens up, swallows up people, cows, horses, whole towns sometimes, then the earth closes back up till the next time . . . never no warning." Daddy was wearing a straight face but part of me thought that he was stretching the truth.

"Is that true, Daddy, or just another tall tale?" I was getting sleepy.

"Part truth, part tale. You gotta decide what is what, Leah. Good night, pretty little gals."

He tucked us in again and we drifted toward sleep, listening to Mama and Daddy giggle in the next room like they always did when he came home.

July was hot, smelling like too much rain, feeling like a hurricane, thunder in the distance. Lightning struck and lit the sky.

Sunday mass. We said good morning to Sunday and saw Micah and Nathan Shine, their straight-haired, half-Indian mama with them in the pew ahead of us. Ruth and I thought at the same time about hot dogs and started laughing. Daddy looked at us once. Once was enough and we quieted, listening to Father Murphy. The smell of incense filled the church. Candles glowed. The statue of Christ on the cross loomed above us. The altar boys stood beside the priest. Father Murphy's bug eyes reminded me of a grasshopper. When the time came for communion, I didn't go, only because of what I thought about Nathan Shine and hot dogs. Ruth went anyway. Daddy looked back at me as he made his way to the front of the church. I hung my head.

We walked home slowly. Daddy and Mama were behind us, holding hands. The country ground felt good beneath my feet but I remembered my red rose box, the pink room, patio furniture, marshmallows, and flowers tucked behind one ear.

I asked Daddy if we could get a book.

He said, "We gotta book, the Bible."

"I want a real book like the ones at Aunt Olivia's house, like the books in the library in Lake Charles."

My request was met with a smile and the next day he brought me, in his torn back pocket, a well-used copy of *Tom Sawyer*. That was how we came to have books of our own. I finished it in one week and after that, when he was home, he bought me a different torn, worn book. He said he bought them for three pennies each from a blind man who used to pass for white. Those books kept the ambition hovering around me. I learned many things from those frayed pages, and though the words rolling off my tongue still sounded Louisiana country, the words themselves started to change.

~

Emma Snow, the girl with seven braids, taunted us after school the first day back. "Who you think you is just cuz you went somewhere on a train? Summer vacation in Hollywood. Your mama ain't even got but one washtub and you's still colored." Three other girls who sat in the one-room schoolhouse with us sneered.

One boy hurled mean words toward us and threw a rock that grazed my temple. "You ain't no better than nobody else cuz you still gotta sit in the back of the bus just like the rest of us."

I hoped we weren't going to have to fight.

Ruth pulled one of Emma's seven braids. "Pickaninny!"

"I ain't no pickaninny!" Emma balled up her fist.

Ruth ducked and I grabbed her hand. We ran toward home. Fast, faster, faster.

"Chickens! . . . Ragamuffins!" We heard them say.

"Dumbbells!" I screamed.

We stopped running and Ruth said, "It's cuz you talked about it too much during lunchtime. You made it sound like a fairy tale, like Cinderella. Now we ain't got no friends at school. They gonna try and beat us up every day."

So I was to blame. "When you go somewhere nice you oughta be able to talk about it."

"Not if you got only one pair of shoes, Leah."

I looked down at my black patent leather shoes. Dust covered them. I reached down, took one off, shined it with my dress, put it back on, shined the other. I didn't feel highfalutin, like I thought I was better. I just knew there were better things to come.

Ruth made me promise never to talk about it again, even if our teacher, Mrs. Redcotton, asked. "Otherwise, we gonna have to fight someone every day."

I made a promise and kept it.

By the end of the week we were welcomed back into our small circle of friends and on Friday after school, Ruth and I, Emma, Lester, and the three rust-colored girls walked to town. Emma Snow walked ahead of me with Ruth and I wanted to tell her about the dog whose name was Chili. I wanted to say to Lester, the boy with the orange kinky hair who'd thrown the rock, that there are places where women wear flowers in their hair and grass skirts. I wanted to tell the three rust-colored girls who'd sneered that one day I was going to make my mama and daddy proud. I wanted them to know that we had been to the Pacific Ocean, where there were no whites-only beaches. Instead I smiled and laughed. I never did like to fight.

The seven of us walked through our small town and passed a dress shop that had a Whites Only sign. The others kept walking but I stopped to look at the cardboard sign and wondered what they had in that shop that was so special. The white lady who owned the shop, Miss Lucy Love, looked up from where she was sitting, resting her big feet, and yelled through the open screen door, "Get away from that window, gal! Didn't your mama 'n daddy teach you nuthin! You kin read, cain't you? Read the sign, gal! Whites only . . . and you sure don't look like no white gal to me."

I walked away slowly but I kept my head up. I wanted to tell her that God must have given her the wrong name, Miss Love.

Summer turned into a cool fall and fall into a frosty winter.

It was December, after Christmas, when Ruth's box came, and I had two shoe boxes filled with books, a dictionary, and all A's except for geography, because I had a hard time remembering the capitals of all of the forty-eight states.

Ruth's box was pink, no roses, just pink with a white pearl handle. Her bed jacket was lavender, slippers too. I found myself thinking that it wasn't so special but that was probably because I was getting used to the finer things.

Miss Lutherine came to the door and Ruth told her, "Come in and stop standin there like a cat waitin outside a mouse hole."

Miss Lutherine looked round and asked, "What was in that big box I saw the postman come here with?"

Ruth answered, "Miss Lutherine, you is a very nosy woman."

Mama heard Ruth from where she was standing, baking a cake in the kitchen, and invited Ruth to go out back and pick her a switch for being a sassy mouth. Ruth dragged her feet, walked out the back door, and the screen closed quietly. Miss Lutherine grinned, went into the kitchen, inhaled pineapple upside-down cake, and sat down. I went out on the front porch and sat there daydreaming until Ruth sat down beside me, rubbing welted legs.

Ruth said, "Miss Lutherine is a nosy woman. She's the most nosiest woman in Sulphur, pro'bly the most nosiest in Louisiana."

I was sympathetic. "I know."

Ruth made a statement in her softest voice. "I shouldn't get no whuppin for tellin the truth." She continued, "I'm gonna tell Father Murphy, next time I go to confession, that Mama gived me a whuppin for tellin the truth and then I'm gonna ask him for a paper with the Ten Commandments on it so I can give it to Rita Hopper, my mama."

I got up, opened the screen door, and said, "Mama, we goin down by the creek."

Mama looked out the open window. She frowned. "Storm comin, I smell it. You hear thunder, see lightnin, don't go up under no tree."

"We won't," I replied. I grabbed Ruth's hand and we took off like two wild dogs, looking for trouble.

We were still running when we heard the sound of a rifle and went around to the back of Hank De Leon's house to see what he was shooting at. It was a possum, just like I thought, nearly dead and ready for skinning. We watched it shiver as its last bit of life left. Hank skinned it, took the pelt, rinsed it in clear water, and hung it in his tanning shed with twenty or so others.

Hank was old enough to be our daddy's daddy. He had a pot-belly and skin the color of a peanut shell. He wore his wavy hair in one braid at the back and a necklace made from bird feathers around his neck. He burned sage, morning and night, to ward off evil spirits, spoke in tongues, and carried holy water, blessed by the archbishop, wherever he went.

Hank said, "One day I'ma make you a possum coat, Miz Leah, you too, Miz Ruth."

Ruth said, "Our aunt Olivia, who lives in Los Angeles in a very big house with upstairs and downstairs, has a colored maid just like white folks in Baton Rouge and a sable coat from a sable-tooth tiger."

Hank replied, "Sable ain't no tiger, more like weasel, little gal."

"Can we have that possum to take home to our mama?" I was growing tall, feeling hungry.

Without saying a word, he put the possum in a potato sack and gave it to me.

"I ain't gonna eat no possum I watched die," Ruth said.

Hank shook his head. "Y'all run on home. I hear thunder."

I looked up at the sky, shades of black and gray, clouds heavy and ready to burst, moving fast, faster, and Ruth and I ran, possum in the sack, dripping a bloody trail. We passed Miss Lutherine, standing in her door like she was expecting company, hoped lightning would strike her twice, and made it to our front porch before the first nickel-sized raindrops fell.

It rained hard for six days and six nights and we ate possum stew. Even Ruth.

On the seventh day, the sun crawled in through holes in the white eyelet curtains and I woke up.

Elijah pounded on the front door. "Y'all all right?"

Ruth opened the door. "We been eatin possum stew for five days outta six and I didn't wanna eat no possum that died while I was lookin at it but it was mostly all we had cept for some pineapple upside-down cake, potatoes, onions, and carrots. Yesterday, we had butter beans."

"Hurricane hit Franklin head on, tore it up. We was a little luckier. . . . Where's your daddy?" he asked.

Mama looked worried. She bit her thumbnail and said, "Ain't seen him. He was workin over in Lake Charles. Be home soon, I reckon. Willie sure to be home after while."

"Most roads flooded, most electric out. I see Willie, I'll be sure and let him know y'all is safe and sound, warm, dry, fulla possum." Elijah patted Mama's shoulder, turned, and walked away.

He drove off, hand waving, and we ate butter beans for breakfast, passing the hours with indoor chores and tales of storms and swollen creeks. We were getting ready for dinner when we saw Daddy walking, overalls muddy, sack full of food slung over his left shoulder. We ran to him and he put the bag down. He kneeled in the mud, pulled us to him, kissed the tips of our noses, and called us pretty gals. Mama stood on the porch, pinning her loose black hair up with gold bobby pins.

We ate French bread, fried pork chops, carrots, and creamed potatoes, and Daddy drank a bottle of beer that Elijah had brought by two weeks ago while Mama frowned. Ruth and I washed the dishes and excused ourselves to our room, where I was reading the second to the last chapter of *Around the World in Eighty Days* by Jules Verne.

I told Ruth, "I'ma need glasses, all this readin."

Ruth turned up the oil lamp and said, "So, Mrs. Redcotton wears glasses and she still gotta husband."

Daddy knocked on our half-open door, came in, sat down next to us, and in less than five minutes he fell asleep, snoring. Ruth and I covered him, turned out the light, and went to Mama's room. She was purring sweetly and we climbed into her bed and talked about hot air balloons and how we were going to go around the world in eighty days.

Mama woke. "What y'all doin in here?"

"Daddy fell to sleep in our bed, snorin so loud we couldn't wake him."

Mama turned over, closed her eyes, and sleep found her.

In the darkness sleep found us too.

Eight

$\mathcal{M}$orning came and the sky was blue like heaven. Daddy went to find more work in Lake Charles.

Mama came to me and Ruth with a letter. Mama said it was from Aunt Olivia.

She said, "I been thinkin on this. I been thinkin on it for bout three weeks. Rain came and I had time to think some more." Mama usually took a while to say something if it was important. So Ruth and I sat still while she stumbled around with her words. "Your aunt Olivia and her husband, Bill, are goin for a visit to New York City, come summertime."

Ruth stood up, walked over to the open window, looked out, and said, "Clouds comin again."

A gust of wind blew the curtains up against Ruth's face and Mama told her, "Come away from that window fore you get blowed away like dandelion snow."

Ruth walked away from the window, sat down, and Mama continued, "They want y'all to go with em."

"Who?" I asked.

Mama replied, "You and Ruth."

I threw a question. "What bout you?"

Mama let the question jump by, a jackrabbit in the moonlight. "Miss Lilly gonna need my help." Miss Lilly had fallen and she was broken in many places. Mama wouldn't leave her. "Some other time. . . . I'll see New York City some other time. . . ." Her words trailed behind her as she stood up and walked to the window.

Ruth looked down at her bare feet and said, "We gonna need more than one pair a shoes."

Mama shut the window. "Olivia been sendin me a little somethin for y'all ev'ry month."

Ruth walked over to Mama and took her hand. "Then why we still got only one pair a shoes?"

Mama let go of Ruth's hand and embraced her with one arm. "Cuz you both got big growin feet, little Miss Hopper."

I joined them at the window and asked, "We gonna have to ride the train by ourselves?"

Mama smiled, put her other arm around me, and replied, "God didn't give you a spirit of fear, Leah." For a moment she was silent and then she told us she would make sure she went to church to light two candles before we left; that way we would have a special blessing.

"I don't need no special blessin cuz I gotta angel who's always with me, nighttime and day," Ruth said.

"How you know that?" Mama asked, her eyes full of light.

"Cuz I remember when you prayed and put her there. Leah got one too. She just don't remember because her mind is fulla all those books she been readin."

I said, "I wanna special blessin."

Mama patted the top of my head and said that most everybody can use all of the blessings they can get.

Ruth picked up a doily from Mama's big chair and put it on her head. She held out her arms and began to twirl, and the doily fell from her head like a snowflake.

"Put my doily back where it belongs, Ruth Hopper," Mama said.

Ruth picked up the doily and replied, "Yes ma'am."

I left them standing there and walked into our room. I opened the closet door and looked at the postcard from Paris that I had taped to the wall. I began to pray because it seemed to me that my wishes were coming fast, the way heat and sweat come with summer, and I was frightened.

Ruth walked in and peeked in the closet. "What you doin?"

"Prayin." I finished my prayer and made the sign of the cross.

"You sposed to kneel down when you pray," Ruth informed me.

I said, "God don't care." We heard the screen door open, rusty hinges singing, looked toward it, and saw Miss Lutherine.

I whispered, "Miss Lutherine pro'bly gonna lose her nosy mind when she finds out that we're goin to New York City."

Ruth added, "Pro'bly wind up in the sane asylum."

"Insane asylum," I corrected her.

We went into the front room, grinning from one ear to the next, and Miss Lutherine said we looked like two little fancy cats who'd just caught a mouse. Ruth was about to respond when she remembered what she got the last time and just kept grinning. We went out to the porch with our secret and started laughing out loud until Mama told us to get out the washtub and the wash-board. "Y'all need to get Miss Lilly's clothes on the line fore the rain comes again."

Miss Lutherine sat, idle minded like the devil's workshop, sipping the coffee Mama had poured for her.

Ruth and I filled the tub with water, then put in the borax and washed, up and down, up and down. Then we wrung out each piece by hand, changed to fresh water, and rinsed.

Ruth saw Mama in the kitchen window and said, "We need two washin tubs, one for washin, one for rinsin."

I added, "Use the money Olivia been sendin us."

Mama put one finger to her lips, not wanting Miss Lutherine to know and we knew to be quiet. Everyone knew that you could use a telephone, send a telegram, or tell Miss Lutherine and the gossip was bound to get where it was headed in equal time. Mama said that was what happened to some old maids and that she felt sorry for people who had no children. I supposed that was why she was letting us go to New York City, Olivia not having any children of her own. I supposed we were the next best thing.

We lifted our hands high toward the heavens, put the sheets over the line, eased a clothespin on each end and the wind blew them soft and dry.

I took one end, Ruth the other, and we folded them, making perfect squares. We washed more clothes, rinsed, hung them to dry.

We ran shoeless between the clothes, playing tag. The air was fresh, grass soaked, clouds heading west. The turquoise sky sat above us. Mama was making bread pudding and we could smell its sweetness. Saturdays passed too fast.

～

Emma Snow came by with her new checkerboard, one of the sneering rust-colored girls, Penelope Adams, shuffling her feet behind her. Penelope was fat. There was no other word to describe her. Even her earlobes were fat. She wore her mother's ruby ring that no one could get off her finger and glasses that had been broken and were held together by a piece of tape. She had kinky brown hair that grew long. Her clothes always looked as if they were going to burst and she liked to show her underpants to boys down by the creek after mass on Sunday. The boys all called her fatso. The girls called her Penny. Penny pulled jacks and a red rubber ball from her pocket, and Ruth and I played checkers and jacks with them while the clothes dried on the line.

I wanted to tell them that we were going to New York City, that we were going to see the Statue of Liberty and the Empire State Building, that we would be staying in a hotel and that one day soon our mama, Rita Hopper, would have more than one washtub. Instead I told Emma to "King me," and tried to imagine why any boy would follow Penny down to the creek to look at her underpants. Penny whistled while she bounced the ball and picked up five jacks. In the distance, I heard a gunshot and knew another possum was ready to be skinned. I won the first game and Ruth took Emma's place. Then Ruth won and Penny took my place.

"Nathan Shine kissed me down by the creek yesterday," Penny said.

～

"On the cheek or on the mouth?" Emma asked.

"On the mouth, twice. Then he said he loved me."

"He don't love you. He just wanted to look at your underpants." Ruth snickered.

I felt sorry for Penny because she was fat. "Maybe he loves her."

"Maybe he don't," Emma added.

"Did it feel good . . . when he kissed you?" I wanted to know.

"Sorta. . . . He kinda smelled like tobacco. I thought he pro'bly had some in his cheek cuz his daddy and mama always gotta cheek full."

"Well, I'm not kissin no boy who gotta nasty habit like that. B'sides chewin tobacco, even smokin cigarettes is a sin," Emma said. Emma was a member of the Holiness Church.

"It ain't no sin cuz it don't hurt nobody," Penny replied.

"But it makes you stink," Ruth said.

Penny shouted, "King me!"

I looked into the distance, wondering what it felt like to kiss a boy on the mouth who had a cheek full of tobacco and brown lips.

⁓

I checked the clothes. They were dry and as Ruth and I went back to our Saturday work, Emma put her checkers and checkerboard in the box, Penny picked up her red ball and copper jacks, and they walked away, looking back to wave once, then again.

We folded Miss Lilly's clothes, placed them neatly in the basket, and walked the dirt path to her house.

Miss Lilly wheeled herself to the back door, opened her

butter-colored change purse, took out two dimes, and placed them in our palms. "Thank you," she said.

"Thank you, Miss Lilly. . . . Thank you, ma'am," we said again.

"Tell your mama, no need to come tomorrow, my sister's comin from New Orleans tonight, stayin till Monday mornin. You all run along b'fore it gets dark." Miss Lilly backed away from the door in her chair and closed it. The quiet of twilight surrounded us.

~

Two Saturdays later, Ruth and I took our seats in the back of the bus and rode into Lake Charles with Mama to shop for the trip to New York. Whites Only; No Colored Allowed signs sat in some shop windows. I wanted to tell everybody in that town that I was going to be somebody, someday. I wanted everyone to know that there were places where colored could go anywhere, everywhere.

Mama, Ruth, and I stepped aside and looked down at our feet as a white man, blue-eyed and bald-headed, passed us on the sidewalk. I remembered the stars in the sidewalk on Hollywood Boulevard and wished I was there.

The sun glared. The heat hovered and as we passed a whites-only drinking fountain, I looked around and was tempted to take a sip. Mama looked at me. She knew what I was thinking, and the temptation passed through me. I would stay thirsty until we could find a colored fountain.

We shopped for petticoats and gloves, shoes and socks where we were allowed, had lunch in a colored diner, found our seats in the back of the bus that took us back to Sulphur, and the sights and sounds of the Louisiana countryside passed. The willows hung low in the heat of the day and the dust from the road came in through the open windows. Few birds flew. We stepped from the bus and a blessed breeze found us.

We walked home, carrying bags. I looked at my mama, memorizing the lines of her face and curve of her back.

Daddy was sitting on the front porch, puffing on his pipe. He took a puff and grinned when he saw us. He stood up and took the bags from Mama's arms, and we walked into the house.

"Gotta get us a automobile . . . somehow," he said, taking Mama by the hand. "What y'all think about that? A brand-new Cadillac . . . baby blue."

"Tobacco got your mind in a daze, Willie Hopper. Stop teasin those girls with foolishness." Mama didn't share his dreams but I did.

"We could drive it to church on Sundays and down to New Orleans come Mardi Gras," I added.

"We would be the talk of Sulphur, everyone beggin for a ride." Daddy smiled at me.

"I wanna yella car. . . . Why can't we have a yella car?" Ruth joined in the dream.

Mama said, "Lord have mercy," went into the kitchen, washed her hands, and started dinner. Daddy went back out to the porch and the dream ended. I stood in the door and watched. Daddy lit his pipe and took two puffs.

Nine

$\mathcal{T}$he next few months flew by and Ruth and I were on a train bound for New York City, wearing black-and-white saddle shoes, pink-and-white checked dresses, white sweaters, new petticoats, and white gloves.

We stood in the train window, watching until we couldn't see Mama and Daddy, our two faces pressed to the glass.

A slim brown porter wearing a handlebar mustache came by, eyes twinkling. "How are you two little ladies doin?"

"Fine," we replied at the same time.

The porter said with a smile, "Y'all need anything, you just let me know."

We said softly, "Thank you, sir," and sat down, close together. I had my red rose box in my lap and Ruth's pink box sat next to her.

Few words passed between Ruth and me until sunset.

Then Ruth said, "We oughta say prayers fore we fall to sleep."

"I always say my prayers before I fall to sleep," I said.

Ruth looked out of the window as we came to a stop at a station. "Sometimes I forget cuz I fall fore I remember."

I told her, "Cuz is not a real word."

Ruth twisted her mouth. "Shut up, Leah, you ain't no teacher."

"I will be," I said.

"So will I," Ruth said, raising her head high.

I took my rosary out of the red rose box and told Ruth, "If we say a whole rosary ev'ry night nuthin bad will ever happen to us."

"I ain't stayin awake for you to say no whole rosary," Ruth said and turned away.

We said one Our Father and one Hail Mary, and the rhythm of the train put us to sleep.

Two days passed and midnight approached as the train pulled into the station. New York City. I wondered what time this city went to sleep. There were too many people everywhere. I looked into the crowd and saw Aunt Olivia. She was wearing a red hat, red dress, and red shoes. Her eyes met mine and we smiled. Uncle Bill was at her side. They found their way to us and hugged us for a long time, as if they had missed us. I liked the way it felt. Aunt Olivia kissed our cheeks and Uncle Bill patted the tops of our heads. Aunt Olivia took my hand and I held on tight while Ruth weaved her way through the crowd with Uncle Bill. We walked out of the station doors and a waiting taxi took us to the hotel. Uncle Bill sat in front with the driver.

I said to Aunt Olivia, "We got three pair of shoes."

Aunt Olivia squeezed my small hand in hers and said, "You can have anything you want. All you have to do is ask."

Ruth told Olivia about the porter and how he brought us what he called sweet treats for sweet gals. "He brought us cream puffs and I ain't never tasted nuthin so good."

Olivia said quietly, "Ruth, ain't is not a word. I don't want to hear you say ain't ever again."

Ruth hung her head. "Yes ma'am."

"Our teacher, Mrs. Redcotton, taught us that and I been re-mindin her," I said, "but she don't know no better."

"Doesn't know any better," Olivia corrected me.

I looked at Ruth, who was smirking, and said, "Yes ma'am."

I looked out of the window as we pulled away from the station and right then I wished that I was home, shoeless, sitting on the porch swing, listening to radio music, watching Ruth twirl in the moonlight. Then I said, "I could be a schoolteacher."

"You certainly could, Leah," was Olivia's reply.

Ruth added, "I could be a teacher too."

"You could, Ruth." Olivia looked out of the taxi window into the streets of the city that was still awake.

Morning came and I looked around the hotel room Ruth and I were sharing. It had a door that led to Aunt Olivia and Uncle Bill's room. Wallpaper with streaks of gold covered the walls and the bed had four posts that nearly touched the ceiling. The sheets were white and crisp, the bedspread, pink and yellow, the floor covered with a burgundy carpet. A bouquet of yellow roses sat on the dresser. I felt like a bird in a nest, soft, warm, and at ease.

Ruth, already dressed, hair combed, red ribbons tied to the ends of her two braids, burst into the room. "Bout time you woke up, lazybones. I been awake. I crawled out of the bed while you were still snorin. I saw Aunt Olivia and Uncle Bill kissin, him tryin to get his hand up under her skirt, her squealin like a baby pig." Ruth giggled.

Aunt Olivia knocked on the door and we both jumped like windup toys. "You're awake, I see." She kissed Ruth on her forehead, sat on the bed, kissed me on the cheek, and caressed the top of my head. Her hand rested on my shoulder and her softness filled the room. "Thought the sandman might be tryin to keep you."

"Mornin." I sat up in the bed.

Aunt Olivia smiled. "You look very much like your mama when she was your age, Leah . . . beautiful."

"What bout me?" Ruth asked.

"Why, I would say you look like me, if anyone were to ask," Aunt Olivia replied.

Ruth walked over to the mirror and examined her face. "Am I pretty?"

"As a picture, I'd say. Leah, you get washed up and dressed because Mr. Chapel is downstairs having his coffee, waiting on us for breakfast. Hurry along." She turned and walked out, leaving the door half open, white slip showing.

Ruth and I giggled.

"Told you." Ruth left the room and closed the door.

Sunlight danced into the room from the open window. A breeze split the sheer white lace curtains down the middle and I played a game trying to catch the spots of sun with my feet. Then I remembered that I was in a hurry. I washed my face and hands, put on a white sundress, white socks, and new white tennis shoes, brushed and braided my hair, and straightened the bed.

Ruth opened the door without knocking and said, "Red on Monday, gonna be hot, white on Monday, gotta eat a frog."

"Today is Tuesday," I said.

"So," she said, "red on Tuesday, still gonna be hot."

~

Aunt Olivia was dressed in navy blue and we looked like the American flag as we walked down the steps and made our way to the dining room.

Uncle Bill stood when he saw us. A caramel-colored waiter pulled out a chair for Aunt Olivia and then for us. We sat and he handed us menus. Ruth held the menu in front of her face and peeked at me. Smiles sailed around the table.

There were ten tables in the hotel dining room. The tables were covered with pale blue tablecloths and vases filled with white daisies. Colored men wearing suits and fancy ladies wearing hats sat at the tables, stirring coffee with silver spoons, dabbing the corners of their mouths with white napkins. The waiter came back to the table and we ordered.

I was cutting my pancakes when Uncle Bill picked up the newspaper and began to read.

"Brown versus Board of Education . . . Supreme Court has ruled that separate is not equal. . . ." He paused and explained, "That keeping white and colored children separated in school is against the law. The KKK's all riled up. More blood's about to flow."

~

"Bill, can't we talk about something pleasant?" Aunt Olivia asked.

Uncle Bill replied, "Olivia, this is history, pure and simple, history," and kept reading. "The White Citizens Council has vowed to resist school integration by every lawful means." Uncle Bill put down the paper, took a sip of coffee, and added, "Gonna be some lynchings, you wait and see."

My mind turned to Micah and Nathan Shine, the truck that had stopped that evening, tall trees with branches. I remembered Micah's words.

Uncle Bill excused himself from the table, saying he had business to attend to in Harlem, telling us with a smile to have a wonderful day. I wiped my mouth and looked after him as he walked away.

"What's Harlem like?" I asked Olivia as I reached for my glass of cold milk.

"Mostly colored. Used to be mixed but white folks got scared, like they do, and started moving out. Landlords rented to more colored, then more, needed someone to rent to. Whites moved out, colored in. That's Harlem," Aunt Olivia replied.

"Why?" I asked. "Why they gotta be afraid of us? They the ones ridin horses at midnight, wearin hoods, hangin people from trees, spittin at us while we walk down the road like we don't have no souls."

"Let's talk about something more pleasant, Leah." Aunt Olivia took a sip of orange juice.

"Yeah, Leah . . . more pleasant things than lynchins," Ruth echoed. She turned to Aunt Olivia and continued, "Leah was bout to drink from the white fountain in Lake Charles last time we was there." Ruth was talking loudly and a couple seated at a nearby table hung their heads.

Aunt Olivia put her finger to her lips, the way Mama did. We finished breakfast in silence and left the hotel.

The streets of New York City were lined with people and I thought of armies of red ants marching toward their hills. A taxi took us to an elegant avenue where there were shops, all kinds. Hats. Dresses. Shoes. Aunt Olivia bought us matching sailor dresses with sailor hats and red patent leather shoes.

We carried shiny white pocketbooks with nothing in them but a few pennies and bought blue swimming suits with red polka dots. I smiled at my skinny self in the mirror, hoping the suit would still fit when we went to swim in the lake water at home on a hot, sticky day.

I tugged on Olivia's sleeveless dress. "My feet hurt."

Ruth said, eyes rolling, "Cuz you been wearing new shoes all day."

Aunt Olivia corrected her again, "Because, Ruth. Be lunch-time soon, Leah."

I sat down in a chair, loosened the laces, which seemed to help some, looked at the rows of clothes, and wondered why some folks have so much and others don't have anything worth locking up.

I tried to picture Mr. and Mrs. Bill Chapel living in Sulphur, raising pigs, skinning possums, sitting in an outhouse, mouths full of snuff, Olivia with a scarf tied around her head, cleaning Miss Lilly's house, picking cotton alongside Elijah, but the picture wouldn't come clear and I started to believe that some people were born to live one way, some people another. Mama would say that the Holy Spirit was going before Ruth and me, making our paths straight and clear. Sister Goodnight would look at our palms and say that fate was smiling.

⁓

Lunchtime found us in Harlem and we sat at a lunch counter, round pink seats side by side. Colored serving colored. Ruth smiled and ordered a hot dog. I ate my first hamburger while Olivia took dainty bites from her tuna fish sandwich on toasted white bread with half a pickle and a carrot stick on the side. We each had vanilla ice cream shakes in tall glasses with whipped cream and a cherry on top. I slipped my shoes off halfway.

The day evaporated slowly like water in cool weather.

The rest of the afternoon we shopped for Olivia, buying what she called lingerie. Silk stockings and garter belts, white lace brassieres and blue nightgowns, see-through red robes, black lace underpants, things my mama would never look at, let alone buy. Ruth and I looked at each other sideways.

We got in another taxi for the short trip to the hotel with our bags, packages, and hatboxes. The driver was as polite as could be and he winked at me like we had some secret. I began to think that New York City was full of winking men.

Ruth poked me with her arm and said, "I wish we was home, down by the creek, waitin on Miss Lutherine to come by so we could throw a rock up after her and scare the dirty drawers off her wide b'hind." I laughed until my belly ached.

After dinner, I wrote Mama and Daddy a letter, telling them that we were fine, wishing they were here. I let them know that I was going to be a teacher, like Mrs. Redcotton, and that Ruth was probably going to be one too. I told them about the hotel, our sailor dresses and new swimming suits. I addressed it to Mr. and Mrs. Willie Hopper, 56 Creek Road, Sulphur, Louisiana, licked the envelope, sealed it, put a stamp on it, and gave it to the bellhop with the smooth skin, who wore a jade ring on his pinkie finger. He winked twice.

Ten

A red, white, and blue boat cut through the water, leaving small waves as it chugged along toward the Statue of Liberty and Uncle Bill teased us, "Are you sure this boat is not a slave ship, taking us to parts unknown or the lost continent of Atlantis? I sure hope we don't sink because I can't swim. Got feet made of stone."

He was usually serious and it was the first time I'd heard him make a joke. I thought about my daddy and his tall tales. Then I looked up at Uncle Bill and smiled. I looked at his feet and said, "No, they aren't, you got feet like everybody else."

"We oughta be in a balloon like in *Around the World in Eighty Days*," Ruth told him.

He looked out over the dark blue water and rambled, "When I begged your Aunt Olivia to marry me, and I'm not ashamed to say I begged, I told her that I would give her the best of everything." He turned to Olivia and asked, "How am I doin?"

Olivia replied with a sly-as-a-fox smile, "You are a man of your word."

Then he turned to Ruth and me. "Make sure when you get married and waltz down the aisle that he's a man of his word. That's the one thing you can't take from a man, his word."

Ruth and I replied, "Yessir."

"Leave those girls alone with that old man talk. . . . Old man talk, that's all it is." Olivia laughed.

Uncle Bill put his arm around his wife's waist and said, "Old man nuthin, pretty brown gal."

We approached Lady Liberty, holding her torch high.

I smiled, squinting into the sun, and thought that I was still just a poor colored girl, used to walking barefoot, catching fish with nothing but a string and a piece of crayfish on a hook.

I felt happy when I looked around and saw land, happier still when my feet touched it.

During our trip, we tried to behave like we were the well-brought-up young ladies that Aunt Olivia intended us to be, and she asked us not to slip back into our old habits once we got back on southern soil.

Ruth informed her, "That's gonna be hard because everyone in Sulphur, everyone cept the schoolteachers, talks like that."

Olivia said, "*Except*, Ruth, not *cept*."

Ruth echoed, "Except."

I knew that as soon as we got back to Sulphur we would again be accused of being high-minded, trying-to-forget-you're-colored, mama-ain't-got-but-one-washtub girls. I pictured myself taking off my country ways, saving them in a place where they'd be safe and sound, in case I needed them to make me warm and comfortable.

It was August. The New York City air was hot and our clothes stuck to us as we drove past broken fire hydrants. Water poured into the sky and fell back down like buckets of rain. Children ran in and about, smiling and cool. I wished I was with them.

～

Dinner was served. Uncle Bill pulled his wrinkled white handkerchief from his shirt pocket, wiped his brow, and took a sip of ice water.

"What a lucky man I am to be in the presence of three lovely Negro women," he said.

"I'm not a woman. I'm a girl," Ruth replied.

"Why do some people call us Negroes and others call us colored?" I asked.

"Colored and Negro, same thing," he replied.

Olivia added, "Same as colored. Colored is colored, nearly white to black as midnight, colored is colored."

Uncle Bill folded his damp handkerchief. "I don't care what they call me, so long as they don't call me a nigger."

I said, "White folks call us niggers, drive by in their trucks and tell us to get out the way, little barefoot niggers."

The waiter served the strawberry ice cream I'd ordered.

Aunt Olivia dabbed the corners of her mouth with her napkin. "God doesn't seem to mind what color skin you wear."

Someone began to play the piano in the hotel lounge. The music floated into the dining room and found us.

"Good night! Good night!" Ruth said as she bounced around the room like a big brown cricket. She settled on the bed and asked, "What you readin?"

I showed her the cover of the book that Uncle Bill had given to me. "*The Time Machine*. It's about this man who makes this machine and goes to other places without a boat or train."

"Flyin in a airplane?" Ruth questioned.

"No." I explained, "He gets in a machine and turns on the electricity and the machine takes him to other places."

"That can't happen, he musta been dreamin."

"Some things come from imagination," I told her.

Ruth put her head on the pillow and said, "I'm not gonna be a teacher. I'm gonna be a lady lawyer."

"No such thing as a colored lady lawyer," I told her.

"Yessirree. Uncle Bill told me he knowed a colored lady lawyer once."

"Knew, not knowed."

Ruth closed her eyes and fell asleep fast. I covered her, turned off the light, and fell faster.

I fell into a dream, a dream about birds sitting in a weeping willow tree. They were sleeping until a flock of crows came, shiny and black. They circled the tree like Indians circling a wagon train. It began to rain and a wicked wind began to blow.

I woke up. It was dark outside. There was no moon, not even a slice. Birds were sleeping, I guessed, except owls. I sat in a chair until I saw the sun.

Aunt Olivia came in quietly, softly, tears in her red eyes. She put her hand on my shoulder. "Hurricane hit Sulphur."

And that was how God chose to take Mama, Daddy, Sister Goodnight, Miss Lutherine, Nathan and Micah Shine, Miss Lilly, Penny Adams, and nearly twenty-five more, in the middle of the night, without warning. Ruth and I, Gramma and Elijah and a few others were spared.

I told Aunt Olivia that she was a liar. "They're not dead! You're just mad becuz you can't have no babies! You want us for yourself! We're goin home next week! Daddy gonna be at the train station and Mama gonna be with him."

Olivia reached for me. Tears kissed my lips while Ruth slept.

Eleven

$\mathcal{S}$ulphur was torn, ripped up with few places for anyone to lay their heads. Fallen trees rested on their sides. Roofs rested on the ground. Roads were flooded. The sky was gray.

It was eight days before Mama and Daddy were laid to rest, in plain pine caskets, side by side.

We walked over pieces of the house where we'd been born, Ruth and I, looking for something, anything, bits of this and that. Ruth ran to me, a broken picture frame in her hand. Mama and Daddy stood arm in arm on their wedding day. I tried to take it from her but Ruth held tight.

She looked at me. "They ain't gone. They just hidin. I'ma find em. They just ain't looked hard enuf." Tears.

I sat down in the rubble. "No such word as *ain't*. . . . They gone, Ruth."

Ruth turned to Elijah, standing nearby, and asked, "Where's my mama 'n daddy?"

Elijah answered, "With the angels."

Ruth handed me the picture. I pulled out the pieces of broken glass, put the picture and the broken frame in a brown paper bag, pulled my legs up close, and wrapped myself up. Tears.

"Why people gotta die?" I asked Elijah.

"They ain't really dead, Leah, just changed." Elijah took the bag from my hand and pulled me to my feet.

"I can't touch em, can't see em, can't hear em. So they're dead." More tears.

Elijah took Ruth by the hand. "Come along now, Leah, your gramma's waitin outside, Aunt and Uncle at the church. Y'all gotta train to catch. Nuthin else worth savin."

I walked over memories and bits of broken glass and saw the postcard we'd taped inside our closet. I picked it up, tore it into pieces, and let them fall to the ground like falling leaves. I didn't want it. Hadn't been for Olivia and the red rose box, none of this would have happened. Ruth and I would be with Mama and Daddy, walking through the streets of heaven.

I pictured the four of us, a family of angels with silver wings, white gowns, halos of honeysuckle around our heads, sitting near the throne of God. I looked down and saw the peach pit we'd planted. It had taken root and pushed its way up into the light. Tiny green leaves sprouted. Its newness had saved it. I thought of Miss Lilly and climbed into Elijah's truck.

"Why can't we stay here with you?" I asked Gramma. Ruth sat on her lap. There wasn't an inch of space between us. My right shoulder touched the truck door.

"Got nowhere for y'all to sleep. I got no other choice, Leah. It's best this way." Heartache hung on her words. "Olivia gonna do right by you and her husband is a righteous man. Y'all gonna have everything, everything."

81

"I don't want everything. I want Mama and Daddy." I took off my patent leather shoes and tried to throw them out the window. "I don't want nuthin money can buy." Gramma caught my arm. My tears would not stop.

Elijah handed me a handkerchief. "Dry your eyes, Leah Jean, b'fore you cry yourself blind."

"Let her be," was all Gramma said. Then she said again softly, "Let her be."

On the train I began thinking about my prayers and not wanting to spend my life in Sulphur. I wondered if that was what had made the hurricane come or if Mama and Daddy were just ready to go, knowing we would be in good hands. I didn't want to pray anymore and I was thinking that I was going to throw my rosary out the window, off the train, when no one was looking. Ruth and I sat there, shoulders touching, across from Uncle and Aunt. I twirled a lock of hair between my fingers, the same way Mama used to, and more tears came.

Uncle Bill said, "Hush now, Leah. Come over here. Sit beside your aunt Olivia, close your eyes."

I stood. Ruth grabbed my skirt and pulled. I turned, looked in her eyes, and sat back down. Ruth fell asleep with her head on my shoulder. I could see the trail left by one tear on her cheek.

I wanted to see my daddy, tall and brown, to feel my mama's lips on my right cheek, to smell apple cobbler cooking in her oven.

I wanted to watch Sister Goodnight rub up against Elijah, begging for a shot of gin. I wanted to ask Miss Lutherine for another slice of sweet potato pie. I wanted Penny to whistle while she bounced her red ball and picked up five copper-colored jacks with one hand. I wanted to hang Miss Lilly's clothes on the line and watch them blow in the wind.

I wanted to hear Mama and Daddy laughing low, wrapped in each other's arms.

I closed my eyes and dreamed about the pink room in Los Angeles. The next thing I remembered, I was half asleep in it. Ruth, who had been put to bed in the yellow room, tiptoed in through the moonlight, her shadow beside her, and climbed in at the foot of the bed.

Part 2

Twelve

*T*he sun rose and filled the room with light.

Mrs. Pittman knocked softly and came in. "Wake up, sleepy-heads," she said.

I thought it was Mama until I saw her thick hand on my arm. I felt empty. I was hungry for love and kisses, hungry for Daddy's little pats on the head, hungry for the smells that came from Mama's kitchen, hungry for the feel of southern soil beneath my feet.

"Mornin, Mrs. Pittman," I said. "Ruth's still sleepin or playin possum."

Ruth opened one eye and closed it quickly.

Mrs. Pittman walked toward the door and walked through, into the hall. She peered back in. "Breakfast'll be waitin on you."

"Not hungry," was all I could say.

"Gotta eat," was her reply.

Want to die, was all I could think.

She read my thoughts and said, "Gotta go on livin, Leah."

I said, "Yes ma'am," and she closed the door.

Ruth opened both eyes and sat up. "Gonna be hot today.

What you think?" She got out of the bed and walked over to the window. I joined her and we pulled the curtains aside and looked down to the street. A green-and-white car crept by. Three girls we hadn't seen before, two brown and one high yellow, were jumping rope, double Dutch, two ropes whirling, dusting the sidewalk, not a cloud in sight. Ruth reached for my hand. "What you wanna do?"

"Nuthin," I lied. I wanted to find my way to the train station, wait for the conductor to yell, "All aboard," take Ruth by the hand, pull her up the steps, find our seats, and get back to Sulphur where we belonged.

"Breakfast waitin," I told her.

"I ain't hungry," Ruth replied.

"No such word as ain't," I reminded her with a half smile.

"I'm not hungry, smarty-pants."

Aunt Olivia knocked and opened the door. Our eyes met hers and she joined us at the window. "Library opens at nine, thought you two might like to join me."

"Not me," Ruth said, turning away from her.

I thought about my daddy, the books that had found their way from his back pocket into my hands and mind. I missed the smile he always gave me as he handed me another work of art. A small treasure. It seemed as if he were calling me.

I walked over to the bed, put on my bed jacket and slippers, made my way to the door, and walked downstairs to the kitchen. It was eight-thirty and I wanted to hurry.

Three minutes later Ruth found her way to the table and sat down beside me. "You're goin, huh?"

"Not like it's a party or nuthin." I put a spoonful of Cream of Wheat in my mouth and swallowed.

"We're supposed to be sad, too sad."

"I am too sad."

"If you were too sad, you wouldn't be goin to the library. You wouldn't be goin anywhere except church on Sunday."

"I'm goin to get books, sad books to make me sadder." I wondered if she understood.

"How you gonna know if they're sad books?"

"I'm just gonna."

"Sad books gonna make you cry, Leah."

"Cryin don't kill you."

Ruth ate her breakfast in a hurry. "I'm gonna get sad books too, two of em."

Uncle Bill breezed in through the back door. He was whistling.

"You're sposed to be sad," I reminded him. "Too sad to whistle."

"Sorry, little ma'am." Uncle Bill hung his head. "One thing I have is respect for the dead."

Aunt Olivia, Ruth, and I climbed the library steps together, a silent trio. We approached the librarian. She was as white as Miss Lilly. She wore the same sturdy black lace-up shoes and her glasses hung around her neck on a silver chain. Her dress was blue-and-yellow plaid, her sweater white with buttons that looked like pearls, her wavy hair pinned back.

I spoke in a whisper. "We are looking for books, very sad books."

She looked up from her desk with kind eyes and asked, "Sad books . . . fiction or nonfiction?" I thought I saw a smile coming to her lips. "Fiction means made-up stories. Nonfiction means true stories."

"Doesn't matter," I said, looking at Ruth.

"We need to be sad, too sad," Ruth added.

The librarian got up from her chair. "And why would that be?"

"Because our mama and daddy got killed in a hurricane and we didn't and we gotta stay sad for a long time," I answered.

"I see. . . . Most books mix up the happy with the sad, the same way life does. I'm Mrs. Baker. Follow me and we'll see what we can find."

As she stood up we looked down at our feet and said, "Thank you, Mrs. Baker."

"Our aunt is over there," I added and pointed toward the aisle where Aunt Olivia stood.

"I see," Mrs. Baker whispered. She put her finger to her lips and added, "Shhh."

It was quiet. Quiet like Sulphur at midnight and daybreak, the silence of the room broken only by the sounds of doors and books opening and closing, the cling of the small cash register as it collected fines. I had never seen so many books. We walked behind Mrs. Baker to the children's section and Ruth started to hum. I turned my head slowly and the joy left her as our eyes met.

Ruth and I filled out our applications for library cards and we checked out *The Secret Garden*, *Charlotte's Web*, and *The*

Borrowers, hoping they would keep our sadness flowing, hovering around us. I saw Mrs. Baker and Aunt Olivia exchange smiles as we left and we walked home on each side of our aunt, holding her hands.

⁓

That night we sat in silence, swallowing sorrow with supper. I looked down at my plate. Smothered chicken, green beans, rice and gravy. I put in a mouthful. Elijah would have said that Mrs. Pittman put some magic in her food. All I knew was that it tasted good.

Aunt Olivia put down her fork. "Leah, Ruth? Your uncle has a surprise for you after dinner. Clean your plates. Drink all your milk."

Uncle Bill looked up and smiled.

"A present?" Ruth asked.

"A present," Uncle replied.

"Is it a doll? Because my doll got killed in the hurricane too." Ruth picked up her glass and took one last gulp of milk.

"Dolls can't die. They don't have flesh and blood," I said, taking one more bite of chicken.

"I know that, Leah. I mean, I couldn't find my doll." She cut her eyes at me.

"You didn't even look for it," I said.

"Did so."

"It's not a doll," Uncle Bill interrupted. "But if you want a doll, Ruth, you too, Leah, we'll have to get you one tomorrow." He looked at his watch. "Store's closed now."

"I'm too old for dolls. I'm eleven now," I told him.

"I'm not . . . not too old," Ruth added. "I'm nine . . . so I would like one tomorrow, with hair made from yarn and two matchin black eyes made from buttons . . . like the one Mama made . . . like the one got lost in the hurricane."

I heard the sound of a train in the distance.

Mrs. Pittman removed my plate and put peach pie in its place. We finished supper and followed Uncle Bill into the kitchen. He walked to the corner near the oven and stood over an open cardboard box. We walked toward him slowly and looked inside.

"A weenie dog . . . you got us a weenie dog!" Ruth reached in the box and picked it up. It licked her face twice. I touched the top of its tiny head. I held one of its soft-as-velvet ears between my fingers.

Uncle Bill smiled. "He's a dachshund. What you gonna call him?"

"Him?" I asked.

"Him," he replied.

"Weenie . . . let's call him Weenie." Ruth looked at me.

"That doesn't sound nice," I said.

"We could call him Dog, Hot Dog." Ruth let him lick her nose.

"Hot . . . we should call him Hot becuz he looks like a hot dog and we got him on a hot day." I took him from Ruth's arms.

"Then Hot it is," Uncle Bill said with a smile.

I put Hot on the floor and he walked over to where Aunt Olivia was standing beside Mrs. Pittman.

"I hope he knows how to go outside and do his bisness," Mrs. Pittman said, frowning. "Becuz I'm not bout to clean up no dog doo."

"Trained to scratch the door . . . what I was told," Uncle replied.

"Hope you was told the truth," Mrs. Pittman mumbled, leaving the kitchen. "Don't like no dog in the house. Only place for a dog is outside on a leash. Dogs in a house is nasty."

Aunt Olivia didn't say a word. Uncle Bill took a cigar out of his white shirt pocket, picked up his gold-plated lighter, lit the cigar, and took two puffs. Mrs. Pittman returned to the kitchen, plates stacked in her arms. Ruth sat on the floor and Hot licked her face again.

"That's nasty, lettin a dog lick you in the face after he dun licked hisself and everything else." Mrs. Pittman placed the dishes in the sink and turned on the water.

Ruth replied, "He loves me . . . so it's not nasty."

Mrs. Pittman kept talking. "Don't like no dogs . . . only thing worse is a cat . . . never know where a cat is hiding . . . don't know how to come when you call . . . do whatever they please."

Aunt Olivia smiled at me, Uncle Bill joined her at the door, and they went into the other room.

"Who's bout to feed him?" Mrs. Pittman asked.

"Been fed," Uncle Bill said from the dining room.

"Lord have mercy." Mrs. Pittman rinsed the soap from a plate, turned it over, rinsed the other side, and placed it in the dish rack.

Hot pranced over, sat on his hind legs, and looked up. Mrs. Pittman looked down and his eyes met hers. "What you lookin at? . . . Ain't even half a dog."

I looked at Ruth and giggled.

Thirteen

*T*he next day at dusk I found myself gazing up at palm trees. The sky was deep blue. Los Angeles was beautiful, I thought. I was walking around with Hot on a leash. In front of the Martinez house next door their Chihuahua, Chili, was yelping. Gilbert Martinez, thirteen, tall, and black-haired, came out on his front porch and that was when I fell in love. Hot barked and Gilbert came over to the fence.

I was expecting him to speak Mexican but he said, "What kinda dog is that?"

I said, "A weenie dog," and he smiled at me. I think that's how love starts, with a look and a smile. At least that's how it started with us. Uncle Bill called to me from an open window and told me to come inside.

"Gettin dark," he said. "Gather up your sister."

I screamed, "Ruth!"

Ruth yelled, "What!"

Gilbert turned, walking toward his porch, Chili right behind him. He turned around, looked at me, black eyes gleaming in the setting sun, mariachi music flowing like a breeze.

Ruth raced me to the door and pulled it open, and I let Hot off the leash.

We weren't in the door good before Aunt Olivia asked us, "Who was that I heard yelling in the street?"

Ruth said, "Leah."

I said, "You too, Ruth, you was yellin too."

Aunt said, "Ladies don't yell and scream so the whole neighborhood can hear them."

We replied, "Yes ma'am."

"Get washed up because Mrs. Pittman is about to serve supper," Aunt Olivia added.

"Yes ma'am," we said again.

We were washing our hands when Ruth took some of the water from her hand, flicked it in my face, and laughed. Then she pulled my ponytail and said, "I seen you talkin to that Mexican boy."

"You saw me, not seen."

She said, "I saw you smilin at him. What was you . . . were you talkin bout?"

I told her, "Nuthin. He asked what kinda dog Hot was and I told him a weenie dog. That's what, nosy."

Ruth pulled my ponytail again. "You gonna marry him, huh? Then you gonna have to speak Mexican."

"He doesn't speak Mexican. He speaks English."

Ruth danced out of the room and bounced down the steps, saying, "Leah gotta boyfriend! Leah gotta boyfriend! He speaks Mexican! He speaks Mexican!"

Uncle spoke from his easy chair. "Mexican is not a language, Ruth. He speaks Spanish."

Ruth replied, "Oh. Leah gotta boyfriend! He speaks Spanish! That don't rhyme, Uncle Bill."

"Doesn't rhyme, Ruth." Uncle Bill kept reading the newspaper.

Ruth rolled her eyes.

After dinner, I took my red rose box out of the closet, opened it, and held the picture of Mama and Daddy. Their smiling faces brought tears to my eyes.

Aunt Olivia knocked, opened the door, and came into my room. She sat beside me on the bed and we looked at the picture together.

"My sister was a beauty," Olivia said and tears began to make wells in her eyes too. "I remember when your mama and I were girls, walking the dirt roads in Sulphur, barefoot, holding hands while we walked to the cotton fields, coming home tired, dusty, and hungry. We would drop our nickels and dimes into a jar by the door. Rita and I would smile at each other." She paused. "I shouldn't have waited so long to tell her I was sorry. I regret that. . . . I'll always regret that. . . . Glad I have you and Ruth to remind me of her."

Aunt Olivia put her arm around my shoulder, kissed me on the head, and said, "You want to talk, all you have to do is knock on my door or take me aside, Leah. I don't want you to ever feel alone."

I wanted to tell her that I was never alone, that the angels watched over me, that my best friend, my sister, Ruth, was right across the hall in the yellow room, that Hot was nearly always at my feet, that my books kept me company, that she wasn't my mama, sassy and strong, that Uncle Bill wasn't my daddy, who dreamed out loud. Instead I leaned into her and soaked up some love. I hoped Mama and Daddy would understand.

Fourteen

The houses that lined our street were painted yellow, white, pink, pale green. The lawns were well-watered and trimmed. On this block, our neighbors were colored, white, Mexican, Japanese.

I heard Gilbert Martinez's dog, Chili, howl and peeked out the window. Gilbert was nowhere in sight. I wondered about the feelings I was having, these butterflies that flew around inside of me, colliding, whenever Gilbert was near.

Ruth sneaked up behind me and said, *"Buenos días, señorita."* Those were the words that Mrs. Martinez spoke when we passed by her house while she tended her garden where hummingbirds and dragonflies flew.

It was Saturday, early September. Aunt Olivia always worked on Saturday.

Mrs. Pittman rushed into the room.

She told us, "C'mon, get ready, we bout to discover Los Angeles."

Ruth sassed, "Los Angeles was already discovered and not by Christopher Columbus."

Mrs. Pittman sneered. "Someone shoulda washed your mouth out with soap long time ago, Ruth."

I said, "We should grow a switch tree out back," and Mrs. Pittman agreed.

It was after noon and she took us to Hollywood's Grauman's Chinese Theatre, where we saw *Davy Crockett, King of the Wild Frontier.*

After the movie, we stood in front of the theater, trying to see if our hands and feet fit the concrete molds made by movie stars, tracing their signatures with our fingers.

Gilbert Martinez was sitting on his front steps when we drove up, and I thought I saw a smile come to him as our eyes met. Ruth and Mrs. Pittman looked at each other.

"She's in love," Ruth said.

We got out of the car and Gilbert stood up and waved. Mrs. Pittman and Ruth went into the house. I waited for him to approach the fence.

"Hi," he said.

"Hi," was all that would come from my mouth.

"Where'd you go?" he asked.

"We saw *Davy Crockett.*"

"I saw that last week," he said softly. "My uncle was here from Texas. We took him to Olvera Street."

The new feelings filled me. "Oh," was all I could say.

His mother called to him from the house, *"Mijo!"*

"¿Qué?" he answered.

She said in English, "Come inside, dinner is ready."

He touched my hand through the fence as we stood under an olive tree at sunset.

"See ya," he said.

"See ya," I replied. I wondered if he would have tried to kiss me the way Nathan Shine had kissed Penny Adams if the fence hadn't been there. I wondered what it would feel like to touch my lips to his.

He walked toward his house, looking back only once. Love.

～

Uncle Bill and Aunt Olivia were at a meeting of the local chapter of the NAACP, the National Association for the Advancement of Colored People. Uncle Bill said it was a club for grown-up colored people who didn't believe in segregation and thought that everyone should be able to vote.

Mrs. Pittman stayed late, fed us our dinner, washed and pressed our hair, saying we only needed a warm comb like Dorothy Dandridge and Lena Horne, her favorite movie stars. "Dorothy Dandridge shoulda won the Academy Award for *Carmen Jones*," she said as she cooled the pressing comb on the towel and passed it from the roots of my hair to the ends.

Sitting with hair still damp, Ruth said, "Remember when the red rose box came and you were dressed up, lookin like Mardi Gras?"

We told Mrs. Pittman, taking turns fast like baseball players striking out, one after the other, about the red rose box, the trip to New York, and how Aunt Olivia used to dance at the Cotton Club but not half naked like Josephine Baker.

～

Mrs. Pittman said, "It's not a box, it's an overnight case. Never seen one quite like it . . . covered with red roses."

"She got Mama and Daddy's picture in it. She don't let nobody touch it." Ruth shook her head, hair shrinking.

Mrs. Pittman came to my defense. "Everybody needs to have a private place for their private things. Everyone."

Mrs. Pittman finished my hair with pin curls and Ruth took my seat. I looked out the window to see if I could catch a glimpse of Gilbert Martinez in the moonlight.

Ruth asked, "Who you lookin for?"

"Gilbert Martinez," I replied.

"He's a fine young man," Mrs. Pittman said.

"When we gonna discover Los Angeles?" Ruth asked. "Because school's gonna start on Monday and all we done so far is go to the picture show."

Mrs. Pittman put the pressing oil down and waited before she said, "Next Saturday, we'll go to Santa Monica, to the pier, have us some hot dogs, ride the merry-go-round. I'll just go to the movies on Sundays, my day off, from now on."

Ruth replied, "So what? Me and Leah could walk all by ourselves to the Leimert Theater on Sundays like ev'ryone else round here. We don't gotta go all the way to HOLLYWOOD just to go to the picture show." Ruth looked sideways, about to say something that had fire in it, thought better and pursed her lips, keeping the words inside.

Mrs. Pittman was holding a rope she wasn't ready to let go of. "And the Saturday after that we'll go discover Griffith Park or drive out to Compton to see my sister, Ora, who I ain't seen for several weeks because I been too busy takin care of the Hopper girls. Then maybe the weekend after that we could try to ride the train down to San Diego and walk over into Tijuana, Mexico, and I could buy me a big bottle of tequila with a worm in it so I could drink it late at night after Ruth dun tried to drive me out my mind."

No words filled the room as Mrs. Pittman finished pressing Ruth's hair, and when Aunt Olivia and Uncle Bill drove up, Mrs. Pittman picked up her sweater and her purse, opened the kitchen door, and walked over the threshold into the night. We followed. She backed her car out of the driveway and we watched until the taillights disappeared in the darkness.

I wondered who Mrs. Pittman went home to, if there was someone waiting for her to put her key into the lock and open the door. I wondered if she was loved or lonely. She wasn't what anyone would call a pretty woman but when you looked into her eyes, there was beauty.

~

I looked up at the stars and the full moon that lit the summer sky.

Ruth asked, "Why you always lookin up, like there's not enough for you down here?"

"Just like to," was all I could think to say.

The truth was that looking at the stars and the moon seemed to take me to another place.

I looked straight into Ruth's eyes and said, "Mama and Daddy nearby, I can feel em."

Ruth questioned me, "What bout Miss Lutherine? You think she knows all those things we said about her?"

~

"She's pro'bly in purgatory for gossipin and carryin tales," I said.

"You think Nathan and Micah Shine in heaven?"

"Pro'bly," I answered. "Didn't have time to do nuthin too bad."

Ruth said, "Oh."

The smell of Mexican food came from the Martinez's open kitchen window and I took a deep breath.

Aunt Olivia called to us from the open door. "Leah . . . Ruth!"

"Yes ma'am?" we replied.

"Come inside. Your gramma's on the telephone."

It had been nearly a month since we had said good-bye to her at the church.

"Comin." We hurried up the front steps.

Aunt Olivia handed Ruth the phone. I stood close to her, trying to listen. "Hi, Gramma," Ruth said. "Leah's right here. We gotta dog . . . a weenie dog but we call him Hot because Weenie doesn't sound nice. And Leah gotta boyfriend."

I took the phone from her hand. "Hi, Gramma."

"Hi, Leah Jean. Finally got some of the phone lines back up," Gramma said. "Sulphur's still a mess. Lord have mercy . . . I miss y'all." It sounded like she was about to cry.

"I miss you too, Gramma," I said.

Ruth grabbed at the phone. "I wanna talk some more!"

"Wait!" I replied and kept talking. "We start school on Monday and we went to the library and we saw *Davy Crockett* and Mrs. Pittman is gonna take us to Mexico so she can get something with a worm in it because she said that Ruth is bout to drive her outta her mind."

Gramma laughed and said, "Sounds like y'all is fine . . . just fine. Now let me talk to Ruth a little bit. It's late here. Good night, Leah."

"Good night, Gramma," I said and handed the phone to Ruth.

Fifteen

*M*onday morning. The first day of school. I was nervous. Aunt Olivia walked us to school, lunch boxes in our hands, ribbons in our hair, brown-and-white saddle shoes on our feet.

It was a two-story redbrick building and I felt tied up inside as I entered my classroom and took a seat. I was in the sixth grade, Ruth fifth.

The teacher had red hair, freckles, and fat ankles. Her name was Mrs. Larson and she wore a smile. Around me sat children of every color. We each had our own desk and our own books. The desks were clean and the books looked new. It wasn't like Sulphur, where I'd shared an old desk and torn books with two, sometimes three others. Everyone was wearing shoes and what looked like new clothes. I thought about Mrs. Redcotton, remembering how she always called me Leah Jean.

Mrs. Larson had the new students tell about where they were from. She said that most people in Los Angeles were from some-where else. Donna Peterson, a girl with yellow hair, was first. She said she was from Minnesota, where it snowed a lot. She said she liked to ice-skate, that she had two brothers, and that her father was an airplane pilot. Everyone in the class was asked to welcome her. They said, "Welcome, Donna!"

Then it was my turn. I stood and said, "My name is Leah Jean Hopper and I'm from Sulphur, Louisiana. I came to Los Angeles to live with my uncle and aunt because my mama and daddy died in a hurricane. I have one sister whose name is Ruth. She's in the fifth grade. I have a dog whose name is Hot."

Mrs. Larson asked me, "Do you like Los Angeles, Leah?"

I replied, "Yes ma'am." I wanted to tell her to call me Leah Jean but I didn't.

Everyone in the classroom said, "Welcome, Leah!"

I ate lunch with Ruth, Donna Peterson, and a colored girl from my class whose name was Michelle Jordan. Michelle Jordan wore pink lipstick and a brassiere that you could see through her white cotton shirt. She was light brown with green eyes. She was the sort of girl boys hover around like bees collecting nectar.

After lunch, Mrs. Larson wrote arithmetic problems on the blackboard. I copied them on my paper and took a deep breath. I looked around the room, watching, wondering if these boys and girls were all smarter than me. I looked at my paper and began to write my answers, remembering that Mrs. Redcotton had said that I was smart enough. Smart enough.

Sixteen

*J*ust as Mrs. Pittman had promised, Saturday afternoon found us staring at the Pacific Ocean from the Santa Monica Pier, sipping Coca-Cola, watching seagulls fly.

I told Mrs. Pittman, "The place where the ocean meets the sky is called the horizon."

"The horizon . . . is that so?" she replied, looking out over the waves. The gulls filled a moment of silence with their song and then she said, "I'm goin to the movies with my sister tomorrow, gonna see *The Seven Year Itch* with Marilyn Monroe."

We walked along the pier back toward the beach, took off our shoes, and walked to the water's edge. We made our footprints in wet sand and signed our names beneath them, just like the ones at Grauman's Chinese Theatre. We walked south toward Venice Beach and by the time we walked back, the tide had come in and erased our trail. We ran up toward the water, letting it chase us, smiling all the while. Then we sat and watched the sun disappear to less than half, orange and glowing.

"Bout time for supper," Mrs. Pittman said as she dusted the sand from her feet. She put her shoes on and stood up.

Ruth and I put on our shoes and followed her to the car.

We drove down Pico Boulevard. I was kneeling in the backseat, looking toward the ocean. I turned around and asked, "How come the sun is always in a ball and the moon is always changing?"

Mrs. Pittman answered, "Because that's the way God made the world. Soon as you get in, best take a bath because you both smell like dead fiddler crabs tangled up with seaweed. Stinky."

I said, "No such thing as a fiddler crab."

"Sure is, play you a tune, you listen hard enuf."

The car pulled to a stop in front of our house and we got out. The lights in the house were on and Aunt Olivia's car was parked behind Uncle Bill's in the driveway. Mrs. Pittman said, "G'night," drove off, and was gone.

Gilbert Martinez was standing outside. He walked toward me and handed me a letter. "Hi, Leah. . . . Hi, Ruth."

I took the letter from his hand. "Hi, Gilbert."

Ruth stuck her tongue out at him. He went back to his house, and we opened the gate and walked into our yard.

"What's that, some kinda love letter?" Ruth tried to grab it from my hand.

"Stoppit, Ruth." I pushed her hand away.

The front door was unlocked. I opened it and smelled chili cooking. Aunt Olivia hardly ever cooked, saying she didn't have a talent for it, and I wondered what it would taste like. Uncle Bill looked up from his paper, smiled, and said, "Good evenin, Leah . . . Ruth."

"Evenin, Uncle Bill," we replied.

I walked up the stairs, holding the letter, Ruth behind me. I heard bathwater running.

Ruth said, "Olivia must have smelled us coming."

I told her, "No one can smell like that except Hank De Leon when a possum's nearby."

Olivia turned off the bathwater, peeked from behind Ruth's bathroom door, and smiled. "Nice day?"

We replied, "Yes ma'am."

"After you get your bath, come downstairs and get some chili and crackers."

"Yes ma'am," we said again.

I went to my room, locked the door, and opened the letter. It said,

Dear Leah,

I like you a lot and I think you are very pretty.

Love, Gilbert

It was my first love letter. I got a chair, opened the closet door, reached up high for my red rose box, and took it down. I opened it, looked at the picture of Mama and Daddy, emptied my pockets of the four seashells I'd been carrying most of the day, put the letter and the shells in the box, decided not to cry on a Saturday night, and wondered what happens to swallowed tears.

I locked the box, put it away, and got undressed. I sank into the tub, put my head under the water, and washed my hair with Ivory soap like Mama used to. The sweetness of the soap, like the smell of perfume, brought a smile to my insides and I thought, Mama wouldn't want me to be a sad girl.

It felt like I was a million miles from Sulphur and crayfish, cotton fields and hand-me-down clothes, a one-room school-house, segregation, and Jim Crow. But I knew one thing. I knew that I would gladly give up this new comfort and freedom to be in my mama's arms, to feel the tenderness in my daddy's touch one more time.

Seventeen

$\mathcal{M}$ichelle Jordan took a bite from her peanut butter and jelly sandwich and said, "We're the three prettiest girls in class."

Donna replied, "I know."

I looked at them as they sipped chocolate milk from the bottles. They were pretty, I was sure of that, but I wondered if I was.

"I'm gonna be a teacher, like Mrs. Larson," I said.

"I'm gonna be a movie star," Michelle announced.

Donna said, "I'm gonna be a mother, like my mother."

"Oh," I said. "My mama was a mother but she took care of Miss Lilly too."

"Like a nurse?" Michelle asked.

"No, like a maid," I replied. "Me and Ruth used to wash Miss Lilly's clothes every Saturday and she paid us both a dime."

"We have a maid. Her name is Hattie," Donna said.

"Is she colored?" Michelle asked.

"Yes, she's colored," Donna replied.

"All maids are colored," I said.

"No they aren't," Donna said. "My mother knows a lady who lives in Beverly Hills and her maid is German."

I replied, "Oh." I couldn't think of anything else to say. I looked at Michelle. She took another bite from her sandwich. Silence.

Someone kicked a red ball across the playground and it landed at my feet. I put down my lunch, stood, and picked up the ball. I socked it hard to the boy who had sent it flying and he caught it. I sat down to finish my lunch.

Michelle took one last sip of milk, reached in her pocketbook, took out her lipstick, and painted her lips pale pink. The movie star.

I looked at Donna and Michelle. I remembered Penny Adams and Emma Snow and I felt out of place with these girls who had never walked to school barefoot on dirt roads, wearing pickaninny braids or hand-me-down clothes.

⌒

The days and weeks passed and red and gold leaves fell from the branches of the few trees that would sit naked through the California winter.

Mrs. Pittman and I were alone in the kitchen on a rainy Thursday afternoon and I looked through the window at a sparrow that had found shelter under the red tiles of the roof of the house next door, playing hide-and-seek with the raindrops.

"Do you have a husband?" I asked.

Mrs. Pittman dropped neck bones into the iron pot with the black-eyed peas, put the top on the pot, and sat down like she was tired. She slipped her shoes off, put her feet up, and said, "Had me a husband once, thought he was the best thing since the radio and Nat King Cole. He got on a train one day, never heard from him since. Only thing he left was a yellow tie. Still got that tie just to remind me that ain't nuthin as good as the radio and Nat King Cole."

We sat there, silent, until the pot boiled over.

Eighteen

Ruth stayed after school one day, practicing for a play. I walked home alone and the rain came, little more than a mist. I liked the feel of it, the taste of the damp air. Right then, I was back in Sulphur, expecting to see Mama's face in the kitchen window, waiting on her girls. Instead, Hot ran up to me, dancing around my feet like he was doing the jitterbug.

Mrs. Martinez called from her front door, "Leah! It's cold . . . *muy frío* . . . I just made some meatball soup . . . *albóndigas* and some tamales. Would you like to have some? You are welcome."

I hoped Gilbert was home as I opened her gate and entered their house.

"Gilberto . . . Gilbert is not home. He's on the baseball team . . . the shortstop. Today he has practice, even in this weather." Mrs. Martinez closed the door behind me. Their house was warm, the fireplace lit. "Put your books down and sit here by the fire." I sat down and she placed a shawl around my shoulders.

Chili pranced over to where I was sitting, sniffed my feet, and followed Mrs. Martinez into the kitchen. The smell of the soup and tamales made my mouth water. I looked around their house. Two green parakeets sat on a perch in a silver birdcage.

I stood up and walked over toward the cage. "Nice birdies," I said.

Mrs. Martinez came back into the room. "*Pájaritos* . . . that's what they are called."

"*Pájaritos*," I repeated.

"Very nice, Leah."

She led me into her kitchen and I sat down at the table. She placed a bowl of soup in front of me. Three meatballs floated in the broth with small bits of carrots, celery, and onions. The rice had sunk to the bottom of the bowl.

"In Mexico, my mother used to make this for me and my brother when the cold rain fell. These are green chili tamales, very sweet. They are Gilbert's favorite." Mrs. Martinez put a plate with two tamales in front of me.

I blessed my food, dipped the spoon into the bowl, and brought one of the meatballs to my mouth. It was delicious. "Thank you, Mrs. Martinez."

"*De nada, señorita* . . . it's nothing."

I put down the spoon, picked up the fork, and took a bite of the tamale. It tasted like sweet corn bread.

Mrs. Martinez joined me at the table, made the sign of the cross, and began to eat her soup. The house was quiet the way houses get when it rains. Chili slept by the back door and while we ate silently, the rain began to fall harder.

When I finished eating, I thanked her for the soup and tamales. She tied the shawl tightly around my shoulders. I picked up my books and ran home.

"*Adiós,*" she called.

I turned and smiled. "*Adiós.*"

Later Michelle Jordan called. I was surprised. "I'm going swimming over at Charlene Cooper's house tomorrow and they said I could bring one guest. Do you think you can come, Leah? They have a huge swimming pool that they keep heated."

I would go if it didn't rain. Tomorrow was Saturday.

Charlene Cooper's father, who met us at the front door on his way out, paused for an introduction. Michelle introduced me as Leah Hopper, niece of Bill Chapel, Chapel and Chapel Real Estate. That brought a look of respect to his sun-blackened face. Having made certain that I was not poor or country, though once I had been both, he tipped his hat.

Mrs. Cooper was as light as her husband was dark. She had wavy hair and hazel eyes.

Around the pool were the sons and daughters of old money, new money, too much money, used to have money. I remembered how I'd scrubbed many days on a washboard, how I'd sat in outhouses where centipedes crawled over my bare feet, and I was quiet in their presence as I changed into my bathing suit and put on my swimming cap.

Charles Cooper, Charlene's fourteen-year-old brother, approached me. I could see the sun glistening in his wet black curls, yellow ties in his back pocket. The hair on the back of my neck stood up.

Michelle, wearing a black bathing suit, saved me. With a bump of her right hip, she knocked Charles in the water and fell in after him. They came up for air, her smiling, Charles grinning like a tomcat with a new ball of catnip.

I longed for the creek in Sulphur in the summertime, throwing stones, watching them skip over the water once, twice, three times. I remembered Mama, the flawless glow of her smooth skin, the tenderness in her touch, my daddy's tall tales.

Someone splashed water on me and I looked around at the faces of colored boys and girls who had probably never tasted possum meat, whose fingertips had never been bloodied by the cotton plant, who had never been spit at or told to go to the back door, who were accustomed to looking white people in the eye, and I wished that Ruth was there. Ruth understood. More than these boys and girls ever could.

I thought about playing tag through hanging clothes, the warm wind blowing, frogs and crickets singing after sunset, Ruth and I holding hands while we ran like two red foxes through Sulphur, under the stars, the light of the full moon guiding us.

Nineteen

I caught a glimpse of Gilbert from my bedroom window. Looking at him made me feel like I was floating in a pool of warm water at midnight under a full moon.

"He's gettin tall," Mrs. Pittman said as I entered the kitchen.

"I know," I said.

"Made some dandelion tea, still hot." She poured me a cup and we sat down. "You got the look of love in your eyes, Leah." She paused. "One day, Lord willin, you gonna turn round, be sixty, sixty-two, like me. Some things took me a while to learn. Everything gotta be two ways, scales gotta be in balance, can't love someone more than they love you, drive em away. I got some regrets but this life has been kinda sweet, not the sweetest, but sweet."

I sipped the tea, searched her eyes, and looked out the kitchen window. A yellow-and-black butterfly teased with its flutter.

Mrs. Pittman said, "Now get up, girl, bout to teach you how to cook, in case you don't get you a rich one, in case you do. Bout seventeen ways to a man's heart. Stomach is one of em. Best kinda cook cooks from the inside, from knowin, no measurin; by taste, smell. Garlic, lemons, onions, potatoes, rice, salt pork, celery, cornstarch, bakin soda, butter, milk, white flour; can't say a house is kept without em. What we call the in-betweens. Smothered pork chops, let me show you."

We diced onions, minced garlic, rinsed our fingers in lemon juice. Mrs. Pittman said, "You gotta promisin future in Betty Pittman's cookin school of colored delights. More to bein a wife than knowin when to welcome your husband into the bed."

My eyes were red, watering from the smell of chopped onion.

Ruth opened the side door, saw me with the apron on, and said, "I'm not about to eat anything that Leah put one hand in." She threw a jealous look my way.

Mrs. Pittman said, "Guess you won't be eatin this evenin."

"Guess I won't be," Ruth said and turned to walk away.

Mrs. Pittman caught her by the collar. "Take that evil, mean spirit outta this house, go'on outside with it, shake it off, come in clean."

Ruth went outside, did a little dance by the door, turned around three times, jumped up and down, and said, "Jesus, Jesus, Jesus, bless me, Father, for I have sinned against the holy one, Leah Jean Hopper, whose cookin pro'bly tastes like Dr. Ross dog food."

Mrs. Pittman turned to me and said, "This child been baptized and still got the devil in her. How can that be?"

Ruth answered for me, "We all got some devil in us. Take off the d and what you got . . . evil."

Mrs. Pittman replied, "I'm glad you gonna be a lawyer. Then you gonna have someone to fight with every day."

Ruth rolled her eyes.

The next day I was walking home from the corner store with Gilbert, listening to him talk about baseball, chewing on the red licorice I had bought. We were standing in front of my house when Hot met us at the gate and Chili began to serenade us with a howl. For the first time Gilbert took my hand and held it. He leaned forward, touched his lips to mine, and kissed me. We stopped kissing and looked into each other's eyes. His three love letters were in my red rose box. Love surrounded us and I liked the way it felt.

"I'm gonna be a famous baseball player like Babe Ruth," he said. "He was left-handed like me but I'm a switch-hitter. Did you know that he was a pitcher too?"

I shook my head. "No."

"I know a lot about baseball. You could ask me anything. One day I'll be in the World Series and I'll smack the ball so hard it'll fly outta the park. Then I'll be famous." He had that dreamy look in his eyes and I thought about Daddy.

"You'll be famous and I'll come to watch you play." I thought he was about to kiss me again but he just smiled. I released his hand and said, "See ya."

"See ya," he replied.

Chili was still howling. Hot was doing a dance around our feet.

I couldn't wait to tell Ruth.

Twenty

*T*he year scurried by quickly like a squirrel on a telephone line and it was spring. May flowers bloomed in Aunt Olivia's garden.

I can't explain to you where time goes but I know that it doesn't disappear, because you can always look back at it.

Uncle Bill had given me a camera for Christmas and taking pictures became my way of saving time, people, places. It was my way of keeping the winters and summers, one skipping over the other. I began to understand why people keep their photographs in safe places.

Mrs. Pittman said, "Colored girl with a camera, land sakes."

One evening, the sky was prettier than almost any I could remember. Dark pink clouds swirled over the blue sky, little puffs of white showing themselves like a chorus.

I got my camera.

Ruth said, "Most people don't take pictures of the sky, Leah, most people don't even look up at it half the time. It's always gonna be there, like church on Sunday. What you gonna do with a picture of a pink sky?"

I said, "Frame it and give it to you for Valentine's Day, and if I want to take picture of an elephant's behind, I will." Gilbert's kiss had filled me with confidence.

I wanted to throw my camera at her but she smiled at me and the feeling disappeared like fog in the heat of the sun.

"You think you're something, huh, Leah? Just because Gilbert kissed you and writes you love letters. Mama would say that you are fulla yourself."

That night I took down my red rose box, read the love letters from Gilbert, looked through the twenty-four photographs of Aunt Olivia, Uncle Bill, Ruth, Mrs. Pittman, and Hot that I'd picked up from the drugstore, and picked out my favorites. I put them in the box with the others and locked it.

"Why don't you just get a picture album and paste em in, like everyone else, smarty-pants?" Ruth asked as I climbed down from the chair.

"Cuz I don't feel like it," was all I said.

"I thought cuz was not a real word, smarty-pants," Ruth replied.

"Get outta my room!" I yelled. "I'm tired of you callin me smarty-pants!"

Ruth walked out into the hall, head held high, screamed, "Shut up! . . . Smarty-pants!" and slammed the door. The windows shook.

~

Ten minutes later Aunt Olivia knocked and entered. She looked happy with a mysterious smile like the Mona Lisa, no teeth showing. She opened a letter, from Sulphur, from Gramma, in someone else's handwriting. The letter said she was coming to Los Angeles with Elijah for my graduation from sixth grade. All I could do was smile, inside and out.

Aunt Olivia said, "You must be special, like the first ripe strawberry. Last thing I ever heard Elijah say was that he was never gonna set one big brown foot in quake country. Said he'd felt thunder, tasted lightning, prayed through hurricanes and flash floods, but he was never going to have the ground shake out from under him and swallow him whole the way folks swallow oysters off half a shell."

I smiled at her. She was like painted porcelain, almost see-through, not like Mama. Mama was like a horseshoe. You could have dropped Mama and not felt too bad about it, knowing she was still going to get up and be in one piece. Not Olivia.

Twenty-one

"You think Gilbert Martinez is in love with me?" I asked Mrs. Pittman the next day.

"Could be," Mrs. Pittman replied. "But colored tends to stay with colored unless you lookin to be different."

I pictured Gilbert with a Mexican girl and sadness filled me up.

"The beans are bout done. I need to go home, get my phone bill. You welcome to come for the ride." Mrs. Pittman turned off the pot of beans and grabbed her coat.

We drove east toward Avalon, turned north on Avalon to Thirty-fifth Street, right on Thirty-fifth, and stopped the car. I'd never seen where she lived. It looked like something from a fairy tale, like a gingerbread house. The walkway was lined with white rosebushes in bloom. She unlocked the front door and we walked in.

I looked around the front room and counted twelve clocks, each different, each ticking, tocking, waiting to chime together when the hour struck. In the dining room, I counted nine more. She had cuckoo clocks, grandfather clocks, and clocks she said were made in the Swiss Alps, and all I could wonder with all the noise they made was how in the world she slept at night.

She answered before I could ask. "Used to it, keeps me company, in the place of a man. One way of knowing that I'm still alive. Can't be dead if I can hear a clock ticking."

I looked over my shoulder and saw the fading yellow tie, hanging on a rusty hanger, over her bedroom door.

Mrs. Pittman noted my observation and said, "In case he ever comes back, it'll be right where he left it." She went into the kitchen, picked up the phone bill, and said that I was welcome anytime in her home. "Never had any children but helped raise plenty, some of em I like to call my own. You a right nice girl, Leah Jean, man who gets you gonna get a prize. C'mon, now, gotta get my corn bread in the oven. Beans without corn bread ain't a real meal."

As we drove through the streets of Los Angeles the yellow tie floated into my mind, staying on top like a leaf in shallow water. I wondered where he was, Mrs. Pittman's colored man, Negro man. I caught a vision of him, heading nowhere but away.

⌒

We had just gotten home when Michelle Jordan knocked. Michelle was funny. Ruth didn't like her but I didn't care. Michelle rushed in like she usually did, mouth running like a car motor, green eyes wide open.

She said without a hi or hello, "I can only stay for a minute, my mother's next door at the LeFlores'." Michelle's mother and Mrs. LeFlore were friends. "What color dress you gonna get for graduation? You gonna buy it or have it made? You gonna have your shoes dyed to match? I'm wearing deep pink only because Mother won't let me wear red and I asked my daddy but he said when it

⌒

comes to clothes, Mother's the boss. I picked out a pattern last week. I'm gonna get me some falsies. What about you?" Her eyes looked at my blossoming bosom. "Oh, I suppose you don't need any."

She went into the kitchen, said hello to Mrs. Pittman, picked up the lid on Mrs. Pittman's pot, and said, "Beans? My mother won't let me eat beans." She took a breath and continued talking. "You gonna wear your hair up because Mother said I could wear a French twist and I'm going to the beauty shop that morning. So if you want to come with me, you just let me know because my mother's third cousin, Jimmie, is gonna do my hair and he could probably do yours too. He does hair so it doesn't even look like colored hair unless you go out in the rain and I'm certain it won't be raining in the middle of June. Did I tell you that Daddy just bought us a brand-new car? Now we have two."

Mrs. Jordan honked the car horn twice. Michelle turned the brass doorknob and walked out onto the front porch, still talking. Mrs. Pittman and I stood on the threshold, looking, waving as they drove away in the brand-new baby-blue Buick. Mrs. Pittman closed the door and said, "Lord have mercy, gonna drive some poor man crazy."

Ruth stood on the landing at the top of the stairs. " 'Mother won't let me eat beans, especially in our brand-new car, and I will be wearing a French twist.' That girl's fulla herself and someone else too."

Aunt Olivia walked in, Uncle not far behind her, and asked if that was Michelle Jordan.

We all said, "Yes, that was Michelle Jordan."

~

Mrs. Pittman added, "Whose mother's third cousin, Jimmie, is a hairdresser who sure works wonders with colored hair."

We filled the house with laughter and ate dinner.

⁓

Sleep came and I dreamed I was the actress Lena Horne. My dress was emerald green. I woke up, moonlight falling like dew everywhere, and wrote down emerald green, in case the dream escaped with the rise of the sun.

Three Saturdays later at the dressmaker's, Ruth said, "Next year, I'm wearin red, red the color of a fire engine."

Olivia said, "Red has always been one of my favorite colors."

I stood on a chair, wearing the emerald green dress, and the dressmaker said, "Hold still so I can get the hem straight." There was impatience in her fingertips.

I turned and looked in the mirror, and vanity hit me hard like sunlight after you've been in the dark. I felt pretty. I felt like the country girl from Sulphur was disappearing.

I stared at my reflection like Narcissus and thought about white cotton drawers and Ivory soap, blue gingham dresses and black patent leather shoes stuffed with cotton, the push pedal on Mama's sewing machine.

The dressmaker brought me back, saying, "Got to take it in a little more at the waist; take it off, be ready on Wednesday."

⁓

We pulled into the driveway. The front porch light was on. Uncle, sitting in front of the television, watching his favorite western, ignored us as we walked through the door. All he said was, "Hungry." Aunt Olivia walked over to where he was sitting, bent over, and kissed him hard. There was more than love between them. I knew by the way he looked at her when she walked away, like his television show wasn't important anymore. That made me smile because it was like what Mama and Daddy had, sparks flying.

~

At dinner there was talk about civil rights again. Uncle Bill said, "NAACP leader down in Mississippi got lynched, the Reverend George W. Lee, wouldn't take his name off the voter registration list. All this talk about progress, I'd like to see some. Something big's bound to happen. White folks gotta give up on this nonsense."

"Fear . . . that's what it is," Aunt Olivia said.

"Pure wickedness," Uncle Bill replied. "The courts think all they need to do is pass some laws. Laws the KKK laughs at before they get on their knees at night to pray."

"People have to obey the law. If they don't they have to go to jail, right?" I asked.

Uncle Bill replied, "Sometimes, Leah . . . sometimes."

"Then why don't they take all those people who lynch and burn crosses and just put them in jail because they're breaking the law?" I asked.

Ruth added, "They should put them all on one big boat and send it out to the middle of the Pacific Ocean without food or water. Then they would all die from dehydration and starvation. My teacher taught us about that. Dehydration means no water, starvation means no food."

~

"Your gramma will be here next week," Olivia said, changing the subject. "I was thinking she could stay in the room with you, Leah."

Ruth looked disappointed.

"Or with Ruth," she added.

"She could stay with me one night and Ruth the next," I said.

Uncle Bill said, "Very good, Leah . . . diplomacy."

"What's diplomacy?" I asked.

"It's when a person can deal with a problem and everyone is happy. There's no loser. Everybody wins or at least they think they do."

I wondered how he knew so many big words. "Did you go to college, Uncle Bill?" I asked.

"Yes ma'am, I'm a Morehouse man . . . in Atlanta."

"Then why were you a chauffeur?" Ruth asked.

"Couldn't find a job at a newspaper. My major was in journalism. Had a few other things I could do well. Drive a car was one of them, saying yessir, nosir was another. I learned a lot watching rich white folks and how they live. I learned how not to be poor. So, I can't say it was a bad thing."

Aunt Olivia gave him a look of love and Ruth and I cleared the table because Mrs. Pittman had gone home early. I washed the dishes and Ruth rinsed. It felt a little bit like home.

Twenty-two

$\mathcal{T}$he train station was filled with beams of overlapping light. Gramma was alone. Elijah's fear of earthquakes had won.

I looked straight into the eyes of my mama's mother. She reached, pulled me to her, and kissed my forehead, the way she had a habit of doing. Then she put her arms around Ruth, held her close, tight, like she was filling her with love or goodness.

Gramma let go of Ruth and embraced Olivia. Tears came to their eyes but didn't flow. We walked from the station to the car.

"Ruth, Elijah sent you and Leah some love and a little hug, wrapped up inside me, free for the askin, whenever you need it. Said to kiss you both on the forehead for him. And Hank De Leon sent you the possum coats he been promisin you since you was knee-high. Not likely that you gonna ever need to wear em, all this California sunshine." Gramma held my hand as we drove half a block and parked the car.

We ate lunch on Olvera Street, surrounded by the sounds of Mexico.

Gramma said, "Never had it in my mind to mash no pinto

beans but they seem to be mighty tasty this way." She put the fork into her mouth and swallowed.

"Mrs. Martinez, who lives next door, serves them with almost every meal, including breakfast. They call them refried beans," Olivia said.

"Mrs. Martinez gave me some meatball soup and tamales one day after school when it was raining but she didn't give me any beans," I added as I bit into a taco.

"Leah is in love with Gilbert Martinez," Ruth said. "He's a Mexican but he speaks English. Sometimes his mother speaks Spanish and his father likes to sing when he's working in their garden."

Olivia and Gramma shared a smile.

We bought four white lace mantillas and drove home happy, humming to music on the radio.

Having Gramma's heart near mine felt good and I hoped that she would stay and love me for a while, love almost like Mama's. I stayed near her all day, showing her my photographs, modeling my emerald green dress.

That night Gramma put her head on the pillow next to mine and I told her, "In *The Wizard of Oz* there was a place called the Emerald City."

"It seems to me Los Angeles is like a emerald city, palm trees standin up everywhere, green jewels in the sky," she said. She embraced me and we fell asleep.

When we awoke, it was early morning and she said to me, "A kind, quiet man, patient, soft-spoken, quick to smile, hands with tenderness runnin through em; that's the man for you, Leah. You too soft for anything else. B'fore you marry, send him to me. I'll know if he's the one. If he don't wanna come see me, let him go his way and don't look after him. You remember what I'm sayin to you. Promise me that." We fell asleep again.

The morning of graduation I stood in front of the bathroom mirror and Gramma helped me slip into my dress. The zipper purred as she pulled it up. She turned me toward her and said, "Bless me, Jesus, but if you don't look like your mama. My Rita, how I miss her, cookin beside her in the kitchen. What she would give to see this day."

I asked Gramma if she missed our mama as much as I did. She replied, "Course I do, but I know one thing bout my daughter Rita. She wouldn't be gone if she hadn't been ready to have her meetin with the Lord. And Leah. You be at peace now bout it or you gonna feel a slice missin from your heart till you gotta head covered with gray. Got a spirit of sadness round and bout you, follows you round like a tail on a donkey. I'd like to see it lift b'fore I find m'self on the train, headin home."

I wanted to tell her that I missed Louisiana and living in Sulphur, where almost everyone knew my name. I wanted to let her know that sometimes I walked around barefoot just for the feel of the grass and dirt beneath my feet. But I could feel sadness coming and so I said nothing as I held Gramma's hand.

Gramma brushed my hair and put a little red lipstick on her finger. She dabbed the lipstick on my lips. "Just a little. You got natural beauty."

"My friend Michelle Jordan wears lipstick to school every day," I informed her.

"Y'all too young for every day."

"When I grow up, I'm gonna be a teacher, Gramma. Like Mrs. Redcotton and Mrs. Larson," I said.

"That would sure make your mama 'n daddy proud," she said.

I sat down on the side of the bathtub and watched her paint her mouth. She took a piece of tissue and pressed it to her lips, leaving a red print, and tossed it into the wastebasket. She had wrinkles around her eyes and her hair was gray. Her cheekbones were high. She patted her face and mine with powder, to take off the shine, she said, and stepped into a blue dress that had buttons in the back instead of a zipper. I buttoned them for her, bottom to top, and we looked at each other in the mirror, delighted.

Ruth opened the bathroom door without knocking and came in. She was wearing a pink dress, pink socks, white patent leather shoes, and Shirley Temple curls. "Everybody's waitin. Uncle Bill said we bout to be late if you don't hurry. Said he can't understand why women take so much time in the bathroom."

Gramma took one last look in the mirror, put her lipstick and powder into her purse, and we hurried to the car.

Mrs. Pittman was waiting for us outside the school auditorium, wearing a smile, a black-and-white polka-dot dress, and a black pillbox hat.

They went into the auditorium to find seats and I went to my classroom. The boys were wearing ties and suits, gray, brown, navy blue, and black. The girls' dresses were white, green, red, blue, pink, lavender, some made from lace, others from satin.

Donna Peterson touched me on the shoulder and we smiled at each other. "Your dress is pretty," she said.

She was wearing yellow. It almost matched the color of her hair. "So is yours," I said.

I found my place in line, in front of Michelle. She leaned forward and whispered in my ear, "I have on eye shadow, can you tell?"

I turned and looked at her. The faint color of pale blue was on the lids of her eyes. "I can tell. It looks pretty. I like your dress."

"I like yours too," she said.

All of the sixth-graders walked into the auditorium and took their seats. The principal talked about the future and how the world was changing.

I thought about the way my life had changed, the schoolhouse in Sulphur, the boys and girls I had sat with while Mrs. Redcotton tried to fill our minds. I looked at my hands and remembered telling Elijah that I wasn't going to be a cotton picker.

I turned and looked at Ruth, Gramma, Uncle, Aunt, and Mrs. Pittman as I rose from my seat. I wished Mama and Daddy were there as I walked up the steps in front of Michelle Jordan. Mrs. Larson handed me my diploma and said, "Leah Jean Hopper."

The next day was my birthday. I was twelve. I was a young lady. I sat on my bed and looked out the window and I could hear Ruth whistling like a bird across the hall. Low clouds filled the sky.

Gramma and Mrs. Pittman spent the afternoon in the kitchen together, cooking, talking, and laughing. They filled the house with joy. Mrs. Pittman played Nat King Cole records on the record player and sang along. Gramma made a coconut cake and when Uncle Bill and Aunt Olivia got home from work we ate barbecued chicken, potato salad, corn on the cob, and baked beans in the backyard by candlelight. I was feeling like I had a family again, like Ruth and I had a place where we belonged. Hot sat at my feet and I slipped him a piece of chicken. He was devoted.

The weeks flew by too quickly and Gramma was boarding her train. Olivia had asked her to stay. Uncle Bill had chimed in. Ruth had pleaded with her. I had whispered prayers to God. Gramma had simply said that California was not where she belonged. That it was too big a dose of people for her to handle all the time, that she longed for the quiet of the country, even if it meant she would never vote, that Sulphur was where she'd been born and it was where she'd be buried, that she needed to get home to tend her little garden of turnips and tomatoes, to give Elijah a peck on the lips. And so she went.

I knew that I would miss her every time a train blew its whistle twice.

That night, I closed my bedroom door and took down my red rose box. I sat on the bed and unlocked it. I took out the pearls and put them around my neck. I tied the white scarf with black flowers around my head and clipped the earrings with purple stones to my ears.

I held the photograph of Mama and Daddy in front of me and remembered.

Ruth turned the glass doorknob and walked in without knocking. She sat on the bed beside me, looked at the picture, and put her head on my shoulder. No tears came.